# FUTUREVISION

## 20 STORIES ABOUT THE FUTURE
## BY 20 AUSTRALIAN AUTHORS

First printing, 2017

0 1 2 3 4 5 6 7 8 9

Paperback ISBN: 978-0-9944614-6-9
Digital ISBN: 978-0-9925201-8-2


1231 Publishing
PO Box 77
Kallangur QLD 4503
Australia

'The future is not some place we are going to but one we are creating. The paths to it are made, not found, and the activity of making them changes with both the destination and the maker.'
- *Phillip Adams*

'Hope is when you think you've left something in the future and you search to find it.'
- *Kathy-Anne Warta*

'There is healing in our dreams.
Let us dare to dream again.'
- *Ted Lovett*

# CONTENTS BY DATE

# CONTENTS BY PAGE

# ONE HUNDRED WORDS
## Nola Passmore

It's Gree Jarko. Senior tech. I don't have long. I'm in the bowels of the ComCheck building. They'll stop me when they work out what I'm doing. But I can't ignore what I've found. It changed me. It could change you. I hope you see this. I'll keep typing as if you will.

It started after Nan died – 12 April 2079. Mum and I sorted her things—mementos, things to use, things to sell, things to give to Recyclo. The biggest pile was for Recyclo. Who wants to be called before the Waste Tribunal for hoarding things they can't use? Mum hesitated between two piles.

"You might like this," she said, handing me a small wooden box. "Something to pass on from mother to daughter."

The clasp on the lid was worn as if handled many times. I opened it and caught a whiff of coconut—the scent of Nan's favourite hand cream. The smell yanked my emotions to the surface, catching me off guard, evoking what was lost. I reached inside.

The box was filled with packets that had Nan's name on them. I peeked inside the first sleeve. Folded paper—three sheets with a strange scrawl across each page.

"They're letters," Mum said. "Messages people wrote each other before we had e-coms and e-txts."

I'd never known a world without e-coms or e-txts. I flicked through the pages of the one I'd opened.

"It's more than 100 words!" I dropped the letter as if it would stain me like an exploded paintball. I didn't want the Waste Tribunal implicating me in this, especially after my promotion at ComCheck.

Mum handed the letter back to me. "There weren't restrictions in those days. You could write as much as you wanted."

I had trouble grasping that. "What about the Waste Laws?"

"They didn't come in 'til Nita Barrett was environment councillor." I'd heard that tone in Mum's voice before. The tone that said the Waste Laws were deficient, though her words were neutral-compliant.

I'd never understood Mum's objection. The laws increased productivity, boosted the economy, reduced our carbon footprint. That's what they'd taught us at school. Within days of the legislation going through, the newly instigated Waste Tribunal started deleting files that were more than 50 years old. Knowledge was advancing so rapidly that nothing before then could be relevant now. That's what they told us. That's what I believed. What penalty would Nan have received if caught? 5 years? 10? Mum read my mind.

"They can't prosecute you for things you haven't written, Gree."

I turned the pages over in my hand. "I can't read it."

"It's cursive writing."

"It's a foreign language."

"Drill it," Mum said.

Later that night, I tapped some terms into the Drill-It search engine and found an open-source software package that could translate cursive writing.

It would expire in 6 months when it reached the 50-year embargo, so I downloaded it. I found the oldest letter, cut it into chunks of less than 100 words each and scanned the blocks separately so I wouldn't alert the Message Enforcers from the Waste Tribunal. With a bit of luck, the MEWTs would be too preoccupied with the overload in Sector Seven to notice what I was doing, but I couldn't take any risks. Within seconds, I had the first translation.

*My darling Jes*s ('my darling' unnecessary). *How I long to see you again.* ('miss ya' would suffice.) *Each minute I'm away from you, is another moment torn from my heart* (delete sentence). *It's hard to gauge how our peace-keeping mission is going. One village will welcome us, and the next treats us like spies. Not surprising in view of what they've been through—brutality, bereavement, banishment. But then I see a glimmer of hope in someone's eyes and I know I'm needed here, to help them rebuild something out of this devastation. To help them rebuild their lives.*

I sent Mum an e-txt. "War on Terror?"
"Drill it," she said.
The earliest documents had been destroyed, but I found a series of 100-word articles from 2031 that summarised the history. An unspecified terrorist act in 2001, retaliations, bombings, mistrust on all sides. The War on Terror had ended in 2022, but it took years to restore Africa and the Middle East. Grandad must have been in the thick of it, working with the United Nations in some of the hardest hit areas.

I kept reading, mesmerised by things I'd never heard. I even stopped self-editing after a while. Reducing messages to their bare essence had been my trade since starting at Comcheck 18 months ago. All computers were configured to delete anything over 100 words.

"Efficiency is key," my boss said. "Wasted words waste time and money."

I took his advice and became an expert. No need for greetings—get straight to the point. No adjectives or adverbs—leave it to imagination. Don't soften bad news—deal with it. Reduce emotions to emoticons, no more than one per message.

I returned to the letter. Grandad finished with heartfelt expressions of love and longing. There were crosses and circles after his signature. I tried to visualise the emoticon that would cover the sentiments, but none did. The restrictions never *seemed* restrictive, until now.

After weeks of practice, I could understand the letters without using the translation software. I carried a different one each day to read in my breaks. I loved the texture of them in my hands, the way the ink moved across the page. Even though it wasn't illegal to read them, I made sure I was out of range of the surveillance cameras. An uncertain course of action was brewing within me. I couldn't arouse suspicion.

One day a colleague asked me what I was doing. "Taking this to the recycling room," I answered, ripping the letter in two. I ached, but couldn't risk being reported by an overzealous junior. As soon as I got home, I re-entered Grandad's world.

*While a couple of the men were changing a tyre on our truck today, Zach and I talked to some children from the village.*

Zach. I remember seeing his name on the back of one of Nan's photos—two young men standing next to a market stall in Kedanzei. Grandad was tall with dark hair. Mum said I looked like him, or at least as much as a 25-year-old woman can look like her grandfather. I kept reading.

*A little girl was sitting in the dirt with a basket of pomegranates—something I'd never eaten before coming here. We bought two from her, and an infectious smile lit up her face. She jabbered away in the local language, inviting us to come to her house. We tried to explain that we had to leave as soon as the truck was fixed, but she insisted on getting us a drink. It was only when she moved away that I realised something was wrong. She pulled herself along the dirt with her hands, her lifeless legs dragging behind her. One of the villagers said shrapnel had penetrated her spine during a mortar attack. Back home, she'd have education, a wheelchair, and private health care. Here she sells pomegranates in the dirt.*

Tears prickled my eyes. I could see the girl sitting there, smiling up at Grandad. I could hear her excited chatter. I could see her crawling through the dust. There was a knot in my gut, like the feeling I got when Nan died. It was ridiculous. I didn't even know the girl!

I only read a few letters a day to savour them. I was drawn to the force of the words, the emotions, the details. I longed to break out of my imprisoned world. He described what he saw, talked about his mates, told Nan how much he loved her, how he couldn't wait to hold her. He asked about the baby she was carrying and shared his dreams for the future. It was as if Grandad was writing to me, that I was Nan waiting for the next letter to arrive. And then there was only one. Most of the letters were dated 3 or 4 days apart, but the last one was 18 days later and had a different script. It was signed *Private Zachary Conaghan* - Grandad's friend.

*Dear Mrs Bradley, Joel never stopped talking about you. He always had your photo in his pocket when we went out on assignments. I know this isn't the sort of letter you expected to receive. It's not the way a peaceful mission should end. But I thought you should know that Joel was really making a difference here.*

*The UN was called in to supervise the removal of landmines from an area near El-Sereh. The bomb disposal experts were still sweeping the area, when two children appeared from nowhere. We yelled out, but they didn't hear us. Joel took off after them and managed to push them out of the way, but couldn't stop himself from falling on a mine. When I reached him, I thought he was already gone, but he opened his eyes and grabbed my shirt. "Tell Jess I love her and that I'll hold our baby in my heart if not my arms."*

My vision blurred and I couldn't read on. I rang Mum.

"How old was he?"

"Twenty-eight."

"How old were you?"

"Two months off being born."

I wept for Grandad as if I had grown up with him. "How do you stand it?" I asked Mum.

"You get used to it."

The seed was planted when I first opened Nan's box, but it coalesced as the weeks went on. Something was wrong with Comcheck. These laws couldn't just be for efficiency. What were they afraid of? Emotions? Ideas? I read the letters so many times, I could recite them. I started writing things down. Playing with words. I printed off communiques I'd written at work and added more details to them. Not online of course. That would have blown the limit. But using old pens and notebooks Mum had kept from among Nan's things.

I kept my head down at Comcheck over the next few weeks, spreading my research out in short bursts that I could conceal in other jobs. There had been talk of an antechamber somewhere in the sealed section underground—a room housing old machines that had been decommissioned after the Waste Laws came in. Machines that weren't configured to stop at 100 words. I had the clearance to go to that level, but not the access code. I had to wait for a believable excuse. It came with a memo. The next batch of historical data was about to reach the 50-year limit. Someone calculated that that would bring the total number of destroyed files to 20 trillion and there was going to be a celebration.

"Why don't we put some of the old dinosaurs on display," I suggested. "The archaic ones that have the *Apple* and *Dell* logos on them."

"See how far we've come," my boss said. "I'll send a couple of guards to help get the old crates up here."

"Why don't I check them out first? A reconnaissance mission. See what would work best for our display."

He accepted my reasoning and gave me the access code. I rode the express pod to Platform-Minus-10 and followed the labyrinth of corridors that led to the antechamber. My hands trembled as I keyed in the code. Once inside, I turned on the security monitor so I'd know if anyone approached.

I dusted off one of the ancient computers and searched for a user manual. It didn't take long for the machine to boot. An internet connection was trickier, but I got there. I've been typing for an hour, letting words gush out of me. New words. Longer sentences. More description. Grandad's legacy. The Waste Laws aren't about the environment or productivity.

They're about control.

When I thought of Mum never knowing her father, I had to call her. She picked up on the second ring.

"I'm in the Minus-10 antechamber."

"I used to work there," she said.

"But how ...?"

"They terminated me for asking questions they didn't like, but we haven't got time for that. There are security cameras hidden in the panelling above the air conditioning unit. They don't watch the feed continuously, but your call's probably set off the transmission sensors. They'll come for you if they see what you're typing."

"How did you know I was typing?"

"I called you Griot, didn't I?"

I could have asked, but I wanted to see it on the screen, as if that would somehow make it more real. I typed in the search term

*Griot, pronounced Gree-oh. A West African word for storyteller.*

I glanced at the security monitor. Six MEWTs were running through the maze of corridors towards the antechamber. "They're almost here," my voice remained strangely calm. "They'll take me away."

"They can't take your story, Gree." Mum's voice was breaking.

"They'll erase the file."

"E-com it."

"The new computers only deal in 100-word chunks."

"But there's no limit on what they can receive from the old ones."

I had no idea.

I saved the file and sent it to Mum, the Waste Tribunal, the Media Circuit, and everyone at Comcheck. That's what you're reading now, but I'm still clattering at these keys. Even if no-one sees how it ends, I have to keep going.

For Grandad. For Nan. For me.

The MEWTs are punching in the access code.

*I am Griot. 100 words are not enough. The stories in me cannot be restr...*

# THE SAFETY NET
## Kenneth J. Johnson

Captain William Flint patted the comforting bulge on his utility belt. It was the latest addition to his collection of space gadgetry. The Molecular Transporter Device (MTD) was the newest apparatus in his arsenal and had many stages of miniaturisation to go before it would become general Space Service Equipment.

Flint was one of the privileged few to have been issued with the MTD because of the danger inherent in his exploratory work. Arguments between developers and the government had led to its limited deployment. The effects on the user were under debate. A device that dematerialised its wearer out of danger at the touch of a button inevitably affected how a person faced the perils of everyday life. Flint stepped into the mother ship's shuttle and initialised the communication console.

"Shuttle to ship."

"Is that you, Flint?"

"Who else, Bud? Clear me for release, will you?"

"Who's with you?"

"On my own, everyone else is working on the damage from the wormhole incident."

"Shouldn't you be helping?"

"Nothing I can do – the boys can handle it. I'm going to have a scout around."

"You can't go on your own, you've no idea what might be out there." The disembodied voice sounded mildly authoritative.

"Stop worrying, Bud, I've got the MTD – I'll be fine. I spotted red earth in that crater we overflew. Could be iron rich. I'll bring a few samples back."

"Okay – if you're sure, but be extra careful."

"Stop fretting. Am I good to go?"

"I could get shot for this. Good luck – clamps released."

The shuttle fell away from the hull. Flint manoeuvred over the dense jungle towards the crimson caldera in the distance. The entire rim looked rusty. *This could be the biggest find since West Australia.* Steel was an overused commodity on Earth and iron ore was a limited resource becoming rarer every year. Flint celebrated the find and put the shuttle down in the crater's basin. The atmosphere had a high oxygen content, which accounted for the extensive rust and allowed exploration without an environment suit. Flint shut down the motor and worked his way through the narrow corridors to the bay containing the hover-bike. The storage bay opened to his command. He flew the bike out into the sunshine of the alien landscape.

The planet was at a primitive stage of development. It was smaller than Earth with almost no magnetic field. Because of the lower gravity, the flora grew taller and broader than on Earth. Flint flew into a primaeval forest of such grandeur that the sky was barely visible through the high canopy of vegetation. Heavy drops of water dripped incessantly from the huge leaves that shaded the ground: *should have worn my waterproofs.*

The novel environment drew him in. He moved from one intriguing species to the next, always spotting another to investigate in the distance.

Getting off the bike, he set the controls to 'follow' and pushed through a dense clump of trees. The bike hovered behind him like a faithful dog.

He parted a barrier of fronds and immediately wished he hadn't. Standing in a small clearing was a hideous creature. Three sides of its body were identical and covered with ugly welts and warts. The sides met twenty metres in the air at a blunt truncation that looked as if it was missing a head. Crooked teeth overgrew a gaping slit near the flat top. Limbs with long curved claws sprouted uniformly from each of the three sides at both the upper and lower extremities. It was impossible to tell which way the beast was facing.

Flint backed away, allowing the parted fronds to spring back with a loud crack. The alien's body bent towards the noise and it slid quietly towards Flint's heavy breathing. Expedience overcame curiosity. Flint leapt onto the bike and headed back into the trees. He turned up the speed, but the monster kept pace, dodging through obstacles as if steered by radar. Flint varied his speed, circled behind trees, crossed water, and doubled back, but the monster stayed with him and was gradually gaining.

*Where's the damned shuttle? I can't outrun this thing. Damn the magnetic field – no compass to navigate by — did I pass that purple tree before?*

Flint peered between the thick foliage looking for familiar landmarks. For the next five kilometres, he fled the slavering creature, staying seconds ahead. Panic precipitated a bad judgement call about a gap in the trees. Suddenly everything stopped – except Flint. He flew over the handlebars and became enmeshed among sticky liana creepers. Landing on his back, he faced his wedged hover-bike and his ugly pursuer.

The monster advanced.

Flint could see a sticky mass of red saliva oozing from the slit in its head and smothering the carnivorous teeth. The cavernous mouth dribbled from an indistinct jaw. Saliva splashed over the duco paintwork of his hover-bike.

The glossy paint blistered.

Apart from gripping the MTD, Flint didn't move.

The alien seemed confused. Stopping, it swayed on tripodal appendages. Flint watched, not daring to breathe as it turned and presented three facets one face at a time. All sides were identical. The creature could bend in any direction; it was impossible for Flint to guess when it was looking the other way to make good his escape.

Maybe the hover-bike was the object of the alien's attention. Still hot, the occasional shot of steam escaped from a small fracture in the water-turbine engine. With each spurt of steam, the alien turned a different face towards the noise.

Without warning, the alien fell forward, its gigantic mouth closing over the hover-bike, plucking it from its nesting place. Tossing the bike into the air; the ravenous monster judged the trajectory with impeccable skill and opened the top of its head to allow the vehicle unhindered access to its throat.

Flint gulped as he saw the fate that awaited him. His hand crept slowly towards the green button on the MTD and, as it did so, the creature turned one of its triangular facets towards him.

He knew he'd got himself into a tight a corner. He hadn't implemented his own survival strategies as diligently as he always had in the past. The MTD was to blame, it had lowered his level of vigilance.

To discourage him from abusing the device, the developers had told him the technology wasn't fully developed. A long and intense briefing warned him it was only to be used as a last resort – only when *not* to use it would mean certain death.

Despite the authorities' caution, Flint had absolute confidence in the MTD and the scientists who had developed it. He had talked to the few space officers who had used it. He had listened to the incredible stories of their final seconds of life. The tales had the authenticity and terror of truth. Never in human history had anyone been so close to the point of death and survived to talk about the experience.

And now it looked like Flint might join the exclusive MTD Club of returned users.

Doubts invaded his mind; *am I too far from Earth for a successful teleportation?* The reactors and superconducting magnets that re-organised the molecules and assembled them were huge, heavy and cumbersome. No room yet on a spaceship for such a payload.

Flint fought the urge to push the green button now before things got beyond his control. His training had been effective enough to drive home the point about 'last minute' and 'imminent and certain death'. Misuse would mean immediate dismissal, court-martial and dishonour.

He had no choice but to use his considerable experience to extract himself from the danger. He would gain no kudos for pushing the button too early.

Flint's hand stopped mid-creep. The creature's motionless body was intimidating. Flint waited for the final lunge he knew must come. The creature stood rock steady in the small clearing – the only movement was the slow progress of the hover-bike through the alien's semi-transparent digestive tract. The crushed bike released a final burst of steam which made its way towards the head and was exhaled flatulently through two skin flaps at the neck.

Flint reviewed his options.

A desperate flight from the scene was his

instinctive reaction, but there was no way he could outrun it. The hideous creature was sensitive to the smallest movement and heat of any kind. His best chance was to play dead, stay still and hope the creature would get bored and wander off.

The two life forms were in a standoff, one indigenous and the other floundering in a sea of uncertainty. Minutes ticked by and the alien began to rock again. *Is this a precursor to the fatal lunge? Is it sensing the air for anything unusual?* The gigantic lump of flesh that housed the monster's teeth moved imperceptibly around the triangular body.

Flint broke into a nervous sweat. He longed for a distraction, some interloper out for a walk in the woods, some little woodland creature hopping among the roots. But there was nothing. Not even a breeze to stir the leaves – only the intermittent drips of rainwater on his head creating rivulets down his cheeks.

*A lonely place to die.*

The next few minutes felt like hours, and then Flint sensed the sticky leaves of the creeper giving way under his weight. Slowly he slipped downwards through the network of vines.

With lightning speed and accuracy, the monster struck.

Flint was hurled high into the air.

Below him, he saw an abyss of dark red flesh and seething sinews as the monster positioned its yawning mouth beneath him.

Desperately, Flint scrabbled for his belt, fumbling as he fell. His fingers found the bulge of the device and closed on the soft green button.

It gave under his thumb.

Nothing happened.

Flint was still there – still falling towards the sticky maw that was his destiny.

He pressed the button again with the desperation of a man who understood it would have no effect. Again and again, he jabbed at the useless button crying from his utter naivety.

In the remaining few seconds of his life, Flint's mind made the connection. Understanding came not in single words or thoughts, not even in sentences or paragraphs; realisation was instant and all-knowing.

Flashes of sentences half understood slipped into place. Niggling questions left unanswered came back to haunt him as the world and all its ambiguities fell together in symphonic harmony.

Flint knew now why the MTD was for space exploration only and the stressed training about *last minute* and *certain death*.

He understood why the reception centre could only ever be back on Earth.

He knew that his molecular memory, DNA, and essential amino acids were being assembled in the resource-rich space station. Giant databanks were being updated from the current information he had just transmitted. The final mission and final moments of Flint were being beamed like a television broadcast to the receiver on Earth where they would be reconstructed into Flint II, a clone of the dead one.

Captain Flint II would walk out of the receiver room and nobody would know the difference, not even Flint II would know he wasn't Flint I. He would believe he'd been saved from a grizzly death.

After a rigorous debriefing, a clone would draw his salary, kiss his wife and feel secure with his MTD strapped firmly to his utility belt.

# GOD AND THE MACHINE
## Sophie L. Macdonald

"Do you think they know?" I glance up from my coffee. "What they are, I mean."

Margot, my best friend, is staring at me.

"Do you think they understand," I press, "or is it all just fake? Maybe they don't think at all."

"They don't know," she says. "How can they? That's like saying your computer thinks about opening a programme, or your phone thinks about what it's doing."

"But they're not robots." I shake my head. "They're more than that."

Margot takes my hand in hers. She glances at her watch.

"Why do you keep doing that?" I say. "Is there somewhere you have to go?"

"Sorry, no." She looks surprised. "Not yet." She lets go of my hand.

"Jules," she says softly, "I understand you're upset about returning Michael, but he doesn't feel anything. They'll look into why he's glitching, and they'll fix him. He won't even remember." She nods, as though she has just reassured herself, but it is me who has lost someone.

My boyfriend has been recalled. Michael is my first experience with an NPC, and to me, he is as real as I am.

The ordering process took forever. I ticked what I

wanted in a boyfriend, how I lived my life, where I went to work, and who my friends were. Then I picked his face and body from the catalogue and set up the direct debit.

"I feel like I've betrayed him." I hold my head. "I'm such a loser. Why couldn't I get a normal boyfriend?"

"You're not a loser." Margot gives a small smile. "I remember all those boys at school who were desperate to go out with you!"

"Yeah, except Mum wouldn't let me." I smile too, briefly, but it disappears with a pang of longing for her. "I miss Mum. God knows what she'd be thinking about me ordering an NPC boyfriend."

"Lots of people do it these days." Margot shrugs. "It just shows you're modern and open-minded."

I check my watch. It isn't time yet.

"Do you think his personality will change?" I say. "If he's different can I re-order the same Michael, so we can start again?"

"You actually can," Margot says. "Lots of people do that. They'll just send him back out to you."

"But won't he be upset?"

"He can't feel anything," Margot reminds me, and the reality of it comes crashing down again.

Michael had knocked on my door bearing a smile and a small bunch of peonies—my favourite flowers.

I knew he would arrive at 9am on that Thursday morning, and I had spun into a whirlwind of anxiety about what I should wear, and how I should do my hair.

"He won't care!" Margot had laughed. "He's your boyfriend now. He likes you however you are."

I had faltered. "But he must think something," I'd said. "He must have had an—" *Owner. Why did the word owner come to me?*

"He must have had a girlfriend before." I corrected

myself.

"They're wiped between jobs." Margot works in Advertising for X-Game, who supply NPCs ("It stands for 'non-player character', like in computer games, Jules"). She had been the one to talk me into it in the first place.

"Don't you think it's creepy?" I'd asked her. "There could be all these people walking around, talking to us, and they're not real."

"No." She had never found it weird. "I think it's a good thing. Lonely people can have someone to interact with. A lot of our customers used to spend their whole lives online playing computer games. Now they're out in the world, feeling valued and loved—they're not lonely anymore."

"But it isn't real."

"What's reality?" Margot had spread her hands. "We plant trees in new places to create new landscapes. We make movies with special effects. We wear suits to get into character for being at work. We tell each other our haircuts look nice to make us feel good. We create our reality all the time."

This is why she is in Advertising for X-Game, and why my job is stuffing flyers into party bags for their Expo team.

I had opened the door to Michael, feeling as if I was ordering a male prostitute. Were the neighbours watching? Apparently, every NPC came with a back story. Michael would have a convincing past, and he would create the way in which we met, so I could tell people our story without feeling like I was lying.

"Customers are often embarrassed at first," Margot said, "but they come around to it once they get used to their NPC and start seeing them as just another person."

Michael stood there looking just like his picture in the catalogue: taller than me, but not too tall, lightly muscular, and with brown hair, which fell into his eyes. He smiled and pushed his hair back.

"This is quite weird," he said. "You work at X-Game too, don't you?"

"Just the Expo side," I said. "I'm not in the main building."

"But you have a friend in the main building—Margot?"

I nodded, studying his face closely. I'm not sure what I had expected—something that didn't seem real, perhaps, like the early NPCs, who blinked at odd times and moved slightly unnaturally. Michael just looked like a man.

"I work in Accounts there," he said. Margot told me that NPC 'seconds' often worked at X-Game in basic roles until someone ordered them again. Their memories were wiped, and they were rebooted with new programming to suit the new customer.

"Margot talks about you sometimes. She even showed me a photo of you on her phone. I've never been set up with someone before—it feels a bit awkward."

So that was the story. We were set up by Margot and he worked at X-Game. I could almost believe it.

I'd invited him in, and opened some wine. NPCs could eat and drink. They functioned as closely to humans as possible. He even went to the bathroom after dinner.

Michael was intelligent, funny, and a bit shy. He told me that his job was boring and that one day he wanted to set up his own accounting company. We joked about what he would call it. His last name was Bagshot, and he said he thought he should call it Money Bags. He made a lot of terrible jokes, and we laughed a lot, and I opened more wine.

What I am saying is, he was a real person.

I fell in love with Michael. Our relationship grew

comfortable and normal. He didn't shower often enough, and he left plates on top of the dishwasher instead of putting them in. Sometimes he got drunk and ended up in political debates with other people's partners. He could be selfish in bed, and I had to teach him how I liked to be touched. He was not perfect.

He would not allow me to refer to him as an NPC. We argued about it once, in those early days. I told him that I often forgot, but when I remembered it was like a sucker punch to the stomach, and it made me want to vomit.

"You're crazy, Jules," he said. "I'm as real as you are. I work at X-Game, remember? I wasn't made there, like in some kind of machine!" He gave a laugh at the absurdity of it.

"But I ordered you," I said. "I ordered you through the website. I picked your hair—your body— everything about you!"

"You might have placed some kind of order," he said, "but that's not who I am. Margot was the one who set us up. Maybe she cancelled your order! And let me tell you, from someone who works in the main building, those NPCs do not look and sound like real people. You can tell the difference—they're a bit creepy actually." He took my hand.

"Look at me. I'm here, and I'm real, and I love you." He prodded his stomach, which was a bit softer than when we first met. "And if you'd picked Mr Perfect, wouldn't you have got one with abs of steel? What's this? Couldn't you have got me better guns too?" He flexed his arms, and we both laughed. He was real.

I tried not to think about it. One day at a time. Just enjoy being with him. We create our own reality.

"What were your parents like?" I once asked him as we were lying in bed.

"Oh, it's the 'are you real' quiz," he replied, with a

twitch of his mouth. "Let me see. Dad had a tin head and Mum had a handy can-opener attachment on her left hand."

I ignored him. "But how old were you when they died?"

Margot had told me NPCs often had back stories involving being orphaned, as it created a simpler set-up than having a family around them. Sometimes they were created as siblings or families, but it was easier for them to be alone.

"I was ten," he said, "and yes, I do remember them. They died in a car crash, and I lived with my aunt until I was old enough to go to uni. I remember the church service."

"Do you believe in God?" I asked. He paused for a really long time, and I wondered briefly if that was the thing—the single question that would break his programming.

"Do you?" he returned.

"I don't know," I said. "Reincarnation makes more sense to me. Like there are other lives I could have lived before. But I don't know. Do you?" I repeated the question.

"Yes," he said finally. "Sometimes I feel as if there is someone there. Someone who knows what I'm doing. Cares about me. I get what you mean about reincarnation too. People who come out of comas speaking other languages. It's possible."

"It is," I said. "Do you think God created you?"

"Yes." This time he answered straight away. "Look around at this world. It's so perfect. We're perfect." He looked down at his hand and flexed it. "I can't believe we could exist by accident. Sometimes when I'm asleep—" he broke off and grinned. "Sorry. You don't want to hear all this. It's dumb."

"Tell me," I said. "What happens when you're asleep?"

"It's weird," he said. "I get a feeling like I'm really far away. In Heaven maybe. And I'm watching this computer game. We're all just characters in it, and someone is telling us where to go and dressing us, but it's not real. The real people are somewhere else, and they're controlling us. I know it's just a dream, but it makes me wonder if that's what it's like to be God—if He's out there somewhere controlling us all—and if I pray to Him then that's like a computer character giving feedback to the person playing it." He shrugged. "Now you think I'm insane."

"I don't think you're insane. You've played a few too many computer games, maybe." I poked him and cuddled into his arms, but I wondered if he could feel my heart pounding in my chest.

"Sometimes I've prayed, and I've felt like it's been answered," he said. He caught my expression and looked away.

"Like how?" I asked.

"Just—sometimes if I'm not sure how to do something, or if I feel scared, I close my eyes and pray, and I get this feeling like someone is talking to me. Not with words. Almost like the answer just appears in my brain." Michael laughed. "I'm sounding crazy even to myself. I just feel like someone is connected to me. It's nice."

I cuddled him closer, and I think I murmured something about how great that was, but my thoughts were spinning around me and I struggled to piece them together.

There would have to be some kind of network for the NPCs—maybe like a WiFi network. There had to be a way that X-Game could monitor them, or send feedback or updates to them—even though they guaranteed they would not spy on anyone. Were all the NPCs aware of that network? Were they waking up to what they were? And were their systems learning and trying to make sense of the world, just like we do as humans, so they were creating religious beliefs around the parts they didn't understand?

I didn't sleep that night. When I was sure that Michael was asleep I crept out of bed and phoned Margot.

"Jules, what time is it?" Her voice was muffled. "Are you okay?"

"He knows what he is," I said. There was a pause.

"That's impossible," she said. "They can't be aware."

I relayed the conversation to her.

"It just makes me feel so weird," I said. "Like, most of the time I can forget that he's an NPC, but then something like this happens."

"We'll have to recall him," Margot said. "We need to do some tests, and maybe wipe him and start over. I'll talk to the Systems guys in the morning—this isn't really my field."

"What do you mean wipe him?" I said. "You mean he won't remember me?"

"I'm sorry, Julesy." Margot's voice dropped. "You'll get him back, and they'll do everything they can."

"You can't do that," I said. "He's not some kind of machine, Margot. He has feelings—he loves me."

"He doesn't." She said it quickly, and I thought for a moment I heard her voice catch. "That's the problem with this whole bloody thing. He doesn't. He's just programmed to make you think he does. It's not real, Jules."

A long silence fell between us. I could hear him breathing deeply in his sleep. What would I find if I cut him open? Wires? Chips?

"You can't do it," I said. "Forget I said anything. He doesn't know for sure. He thinks some guy at X-Game is God."

"We have to recall him," she said. "Please try to

understand. They're all built to be recalled. I'll flag his code in the morning, and he'll take himself to Brad at Systems at the allocated time." She sounded tired. "We've had a few recalls for this kind of thing. The problem is they're built to keep learning, so I guess it's inevitable that one day they'll learn what they are. You'll have him back in a couple of days."

"But I want him," I said, "not something that just looks like him."

"Jules, there is no him." Margot spoke softly, and I could barely hear her. "He is just something that looks like him. Have you got work tomorrow? Can you meet me for a coffee in the lobby?"

"Everyone's at ComiCon." I work in the bowels of an X-Game annexe. I'd barely be missed if the office was full. "I can get out about ten."

"What do you think they're doing to him?" I ask.

"Diagnostics." Margot shrugs. "I told you it's not my area. They'll run a load of tests to make sure nothing's shorting out, and there are no viruses. Brad said the problem is NPCs are just too good these days. They're doing what they're meant to do—which is to learn and process what they find, but because their processing power is superior to that of humans, we don't know what would happen if they figure it all out." She smiles gently. "Wouldn't be great PR if X-Game were found to be responsible for the uprising of the machines."

"How many of them do you think there are?" I scan the lobby. Suited people walk back and forth, buying coffees and newspapers, nodding greetings, laughing with each other. Who is real?

"Numbers are capped," Margot says. "We have to adhere to a strict ratio of PCs to NPCs. There's some pretty tight legislation around it." She taps her fingers on the table and glances at her watch. "Anyway, half the time the NPCs are better humans than the PCs. Did you know that there are no recorded incidences of NPCs committing crimes?" She chews at her lip and looks down at the table.

I check my watch. It's time.

"Sorry, Margot, I've got to go," I say.

She nods, as if she was expecting it, and stands with me. She gives me a sudden hug.

"I'm okay," I say, half meaning it. "I'm sure Michael will be okay."

"This part always sucks," she says.

"I guess it's just what happens when you get feelings for an NPC," I say.

"Sometimes it's hard not to," she says.

"I've got to go." I nod towards the lifts. "I have to drop some expo merchandise off to Brad at the Systems team. Hey, maybe I'll see Michael up there!"

"Maybe," Margot says.

"See you for drinks after work?" I say.

"Call me when you're free," she says.

I press the button to call the lift. I'm not sure if it's the light, but it looks as if Margot is crying. I want to say something to her but the lift comes and I step in. I check my watch again. It's very important that I go to Brad at Systems now. I will talk to Margot later.

# A SHRINKING STAR MAP
## Greg Peake

An explosion overhead snapped Trooper 25-57 out of his daze. He was standing in the middle of the street, transfixed by a pile of smoking bodies. Innocent civilians - the latest victims of an artillery barrage. Trooper 25-57 had no time to mourn the slaughter as the thunderous sound of a fresh barrage echoed in the distance. Determined not to get blown apart, he ran for the building that sheltered the rest of his military unit. They were dressed in camouflage clothing and body armour, coloured black and deep purple. They seemed so far away as the bombs reached their target, engulfing him in explosions and debris. Trooper 25-57 sprinted towards the building where he stopped to catch his breath.

All eyes were on him.

"What the hell were you doing Five-Seven? We're supposed to be waiting for new orders – not standing around trying to get ourselves killed."

He said nothing.

Taking a seat in the corner, shaken from the bombing that had almost blasted him skyward, Five-Seven reflected on the events that had led him to this point. He once worked on a rig that extracted planetary minerals, which would later be refined and used as fuel. It was his job on the rig to operate the drill, which used advanced and highly focused lasers to cut minerals from the planet with surgical precision.

Five-Seven would never forget the day the ship landed.

He was on the rig drilling into the rock, when something from the sky caught his attention. His reaction was not unlike the previous moment on the street – he'd stood in shock amongst his fellow drillers, as a city-sized metallic structure descended from the sky. The sound of it breaking through the atmosphere could be heard for miles. The ground trembled and clouds dissipated as if preparing for the ship's touchdown.

Interstellar space travel had been possible for many years, but the ship's arrival was still a wonder to behold. The enormous ship was nothing like anyone had seen before. Its design did not resemble any of the space crafts that regularly landed for tourism and trading purposes. For several days it remained dormant.

It didn't take long for Five-Seven and the rest of the planet to discover the mysterious space ship's purpose when it opened up and spewed out thousands of smaller flying craft and drop pods.

It was an extra-terrestrial invasion force.

From that moment on, life flew by like a blur. Five-Seven and many other able-bodied individuals were rounded up to protect the planet. He was given a standard issue rifle – a military weapon designed to fire devastating beams of concentrated plasma energy. He was also given military clothing, military training and a military identification: Trooper 25-57.

The planet's inhabitants moved quickly to oppose the threat, but the alien invaders had emerged much faster and with more aggression, moving swiftly across the planet's continents and major cities. Five-Seven and his fellow soldiers hopelessly fought on, forced to witness the devastation the invaders left behind. Buildings were destroyed and civilians were massacred. Wherever these aliens had come from, they were determined to destroy everything in their path. After descending from space, the invaders seemed to view any indigenous life form or structure as a personal insult; an atrocity that needed to be eradicated. But for what purpose? Five-Seven could never figure it out. All he could do was try his best to protect his home and its inhabitants amidst the slaughter.

The chaos continued for months with no sign of slowing – buildings were turned to rubble and civilians shot to death with alien energy weapons. Five-Seven and whatever resistance were left could barely hold on.

"Alright, let's move out!"

Five-Seven snapped to attention at the command. He fell in with the other troopers.

"Listen up," the unit leader barked, "I've just got word that a large force of alien hostiles is coming this way."

Most likely to finish off the city... and us, Five-Seven thought.

"We're to join up with the other units and hold them back for as long as possible."

No one said a thing. The mission was self-explanatory: Hold your ground. Keep firing until they stop coming... or until you can't fire anymore.

Several thousand troopers made ready along the city's edge. Gun placements, light artillery and sandbag barriers were built along the exposed ground. The alien ship mocked them, standing defiantly in the distance.

It was silent for almost an hour, and Five-Seven wondered if anything was going to happen. A single red bolt of energy blasted into a nearby sandbag, sending a cloud of dust into the air. The unit leader ignited a flare and threw it as far as he could. Its bright light fought back the night's darkness, allowing the troopers to see the battlefield.

Five-Seven preferred the dark. The light revealed a massive force of alien soldiers moving silently and deliberately towards them. They moved with frightening efficiency and carried energy-based weapons, similar to the ones Five-Seven and the other troopers carried. Their slow and precise advance quickened into a full charge once they realised they had been spotted.

It frightened Five-Seven to see that the aliens' appearance was similar to his own. They stood upright and had a pair of legs and arms. Although their skin varied in colour their anatomy and physiology seemed the same.

When the order to open fire was called, Five-Seven didn't hesitate. Taking aim, he fired his weapon and kept firing until it felt hot in his hands.

The aliens reciprocated immediately, firing their weapons in a continuous barrage. All visibility was sucked away and replaced with a haze of energy bolts and smoke. Explosions and the unmistakable 'zwoosh' of discharging weapons rang in Five-Seven's ears. He could feel the loose ground underneath him kicking up in the maelstrom. Rocks and dirt smashed against his helmet and fell into his armour. It was like being buried alive.

Every second felt like a minute. Every minute felt like an hour. Five-Seven held his ground, firing wildly at anything that resembled an alien invader. All around him, he could hear cries of pain and the gurgling of those who had been shot and only had seconds to live. Rubble and broken sandbags blanketed the air in front of him like smog, leaving brightly coloured rifle blasts the only visible sight as they tore through the thick curtain of dust.

"Fall back!" someone cried, "there's too many. Pull back into the city and take up positions. Don't let them get to the mine!"

Five-Seven stopped firing. The mine. The site where he used to work as a driller. It contained precious minerals that would eventually become fuel, and it was located on the other side of the city.

Was this what it was all about? There was no denying that the planet was rich with valuable resources, but was the death and destruction really motivated by something so simple?

There was no time to ponder. The trooper standing closest to Five-Seven violently jerked backwards as an energy blast buried itself in her chest. It was time to fall back. Five-Seven turned to run but stopped when he heard something above the chaos.

"Help me."

He looked back and saw a fellow trooper out in the field. Somehow he had advanced past their own line and was now lying, wounded, between the city and the advancing enemy. Without thinking, Five-Seven dropped to the ground. Keeping low to avoid the heavy fire, he crawled towards the sounds of the suffering trooper. It was slow going but he eventually made it. By the time Five-Seven rolled him over, it was obvious that he was too late. The trooper was dead - his clothes were soaked in blood. Five-Seven cursed, wondering how he would make it back to the city's border and to relative safety with the rest of his unit. He was now caught in the open, with nothing but a dead body as cover.

There was no other option. He began crawling, determined to make it back to his own lines. Beams of fire flew through the air above him, singeing the air that entered his nostrils. Luck was on his side as he spotted cover in the distance – an abandoned sandbag gun placement. He crawled manically towards it. At least with some protection, he could hold them off until it was safe to fall back farther.

It was wishful thinking.

A bright red energy bolt tore through his calf and continued through his arm. It was enough to make him howl in agony but Five-Seven pushed through the pain, making it to safety behind the barrier. He rolled over and returned fire, dropping several aliens as they slowly advanced on his position. There was hope yet, he thought, as his well-placed shots continued to hammer the enemy invaders. Five-Seven was determined to keep them at bay for as long as possible.

There was a low rumble. It was the same familiar rumbling that had occurred when the first alien ship landed. Five-Seven realised his luck—and hope—had run out.

Coming down from the sky were hundreds of spacecraft, almost identical to the first alien ship that had landed several months ago. However, there was something very different about them. These ships had strange machinery attached, and it took Five-Seven a minute to figure out what they were for.

His face dropped. The machinery attached to the descending ships may have been extra-terrestrial in nature, but as a former driller, it was hard not to spot the similarities to the equipment he used to operate.

They were mining ships.

Each ship was equipped with massive laser drilling machinery, capable of tearing through a planet's surface and extracting whatever resource it was after. Five-Seven knew that his planet was ripe with precious resources, and it was now clear that the planet's resources were what these aliens were after. He supposed the last few months made sense in a sick and twisted way – annihilate the indigenous population and its infrastructure, then walk in and take whatever was wanted.

When the closest drilling ship landed, Five-Seven could see its grotesque machinery, which seemed inexplicably eager to tear into the planet's surface. Bleeding heavily and lacking the will to continue, Five-Seven watched the ship land safely against a backdrop of heavy artillery, illuminating the night sky. He was just able to make out the strange symbols E-A-R-T-H on the mining ship's hull.

# PROFILE
## Duncan Richardson

I got sick and started to disappear. It can happen to anyone, if you're not careful.

My key card wouldn't open the front door of my building. It was raining. I huddled under the overhang with my collar turned up, trying to think. If they'd updated the cards then the bastards hadn't told me. I couldn't remember any messages about that. But with being sick I hadn't checked anything online for a week or two.

Cars swished by behind me, going somewhere, sounding important. I tried again, swiping the card through the groove. The indicator light didn't even blink. It was as if I'd tickled it with a feather.

I tried kicking the door but that just made a hollow boom in the space behind, like an empty tomb. I'd call it a lobby except it's just a few square metres of tiled floor and a lift. I turned around and faced the street, shrugging as if it wasn't so bad. As if my brain wasn't already predicting a night on the streets, huddling under a bridge to stay dry. But I was running through ideas. Who I could call. Where I could go.

I tried the door again, grinding my card into the mechanism, hoping to hurt it, make it pay for this humiliation and inconvenience. Still nothing. I took out my phone and glanced at its blank screen. It had been blank for how long? A day? Two? It was hard to say. Hadn't noticed. I'd been busy. Sleeping. Throwing up. Sleeping again.

Anyway, I didn't want to panic. I wasn't going to spend the night on a park bench, call a friend or go to a refuge. I'd get into my flat. No question.

But I was starting to feel self-conscious, lurking by the door. People would think I was a mugger. Or brain-hacker. They'd call the cops and then I'd have to explain... It might take hours to sort that out.

A gust blew a shower of raindrops into my face.

Shit! I closed my eyes, tasting the water on my lips. It tasted like petrol.

Something clicked behind the door. I stepped back to it and flourished my card. The door opened and I grabbed it, trying not to grin like a maniac at the couple coming out. They were young, dressed up, heading for a night out. Not like me.

"Thanks," said the woman.

I nodded, hurried through and let the door close behind me. It sighed on its springs like a weary ghost.

As I stepped towards the lift, a cold thought jabbed me. What if the lift doesn't work for me either? I pressed the button and a bell rang as if I'd won some kind of prize. The lift hummed, clunked and the doors opened. I stepped in, scanned my card and pressed my floor number. Eleven. Held my breath.

I could almost hear a signal travelling through the system, asking the great brain at its core; was I worthy? Should I be allowed to ride to my floor? Or...?

The doors closed. Up we went.

When I stepped out my throat was already drying at the prospect of fighting with another lock. Another mechanism that refused to do its job and let me in. I held my card like a razor, my fingers sweating as I imagined how I would feel if it refused me. Spending the night in the corridor would be dry but still uncomfortable and embarrassing if anyone saw me.

I reached my flat and held my breath, offering my card, more like a communion wafer now than a weapon.

Click!

I was in.

So just a fault with the front door then. I'd only have to contact the caretaker and all would be well. I hadn't been on *Brethpad* for ages either. I made a mental note to do that on the weekend. My friends were probably thinking I'd crashed or frozen.

Next morning, trying to log on at work, I got one of those little message boxes: *Password and identity not recognised.*

It was like looking into the abyss.

I called my boss. At least she knew me.

"Call I.T.," she said.

I did. And listened to a recorded message telling me that my call was valued and they would attend to it as soon as possible. After I'd heard it fifteen times, I hung up.

Right, I thought. Go and see them. I swiped my card in the lift. Ping! But down we went to the ground floor. The door opened and nothing I could do would make it close again and take me back to the seventh floor. I groaned. I'd have to walk back up the stairs. My knees trembled at the thought. Hadn't done exercise like that since... I'd have to do it in stages.

I stepped out and looked around. A flickering fluoro tube lit a grey cement corridor that led to a green door which said 'Fire Exit'. At least it didn't say it was alarmed. Though I was, slightly. I put my card in my shirt pocket and walked towards the door.

It had an old fashioned handle. I pushed it down, feeling grains of painted-over rust beneath my fingers. The door swung open and I realised I'd been holding my breath. Traffic noise flared around me. I was in a narrow lane. Another high-rise presented its grey flank. I walked towards the street, tempted at the corner to forget about work and go to a café. No one would notice. But I would've felt guilty so that would've spoiled it. I turned away from the shops and headed for the entrance.

The front of my building was like an antlion trap made of glass. The windows angled in, funnelling everyone towards a double set of doors. It was quiet. Mid-morning. Not even the odd smoker anymore. Not since they brought in the Klensing Rooms. Like large fish tanks without the fake plants.

I strode up to the doors and pushed my card in.

Nothing.

I recalled how I'd got into the block first thing. It was easy. I'd just been part of the crowd of office workers. To speed things up, the doors stayed open, watched by the security guard who nodded at everyone with a frown that looked like he suspected all of us of being potential terrorists.

Maybe he was right. I felt like blowing something up at that moment.

My arms felt cold. I sensed the great tower of the building looming over me. Again and again, I jabbed my card into the mechanism. No response. I stepped back, tensed, looked around then swung my foot up. Thud!

Beep! Beep! Beep!

An orange light above the door started flashing. A man in a dark blue uniform emerged from a room inside the reception area and hurried towards me. He raised his hand.

I waved back. "Carlos!" I shouted. "It's me. My card won't work. Can you let me in, please?"

He made a shooing motion. His words were muffled through the glass but I got the gist.

"Piss off mate, before I call the cops."

He didn't know me. After five years of greetings and the odd chat about football while waiting for the lift. He supported Real Madrid. His dad was Spanish. I always remembered his name.

He glared at me. I turned away and closed my eyes. Maybe it was just a bad dream. When I opened them, everything would be back to normal.

Carlos had disappeared back into his office. I was stuck outside. I put my hands in my pockets. And touched a cool, hard thing.

My phone! How had I forgotten that? I touched the screen. *Print not recognised,* it said. Shit! I tried every finger and thumb, pressing hard but it rejected me every time. Even licked it, hoping no one was looking.

I wandered off, feeling like one of those inflatable advertising dummies with a slow puncture. They always scared me when I was a kid. The image of these skinny giants with anxious faces, vainly struggling to get away from some invisible threat, arms flailing, bodies twisting, falling. Rising again.

So, I thought. Have a break. Maybe I could come back around knocking off time and catch people leaving. Then I could get a new key card and get back to my workstation tomorrow.

The idea of coffee suddenly felt good. It would be a reward, I thought. For perseverance. I strolled along the street, reaching a café zone. It was like wagging school with the best excuse. No one could blame me. And I'd have something to eat as well. I chose a café with tables outside. *Soshul,* it was called. A few other people were there, sitting alone with their tabs, caressing the screens like lovers. I shuddered.

A huge lemon meringue squatted in the glass cabinet so I ordered a piece of that, just to take my mind off things. Get a good hit of sugar. And vitamin C of course. Almost a health food. The young guy behind the counter had a shaved head with a tattoo over his left ear. *No buffering.* And a small blue wheel with a cross through it. I thought of the time and pain he must've gone through, to get it.

When I swiped my cash card, the guy looked at the register screen. "Sorry mate," he said. "The machine doesn't like it."

"What?"

He swung the screen around. *Not recognised,* it said.

My stomach lurched.

"Are you okay?" the guy said.

I hurried away.

Two hours later, I was sitting in the gardens. At least you don't need an access card for that. Not yet anyway. It was mid-afternoon. Lunchtime picnickers were packing up. Kids were feeding ducks. A light blue van rolled down the road that ran through the park, beneath the huge and ancient Moreton Bay figs. As it slipped by me, I noticed it had *ProSup* in bright red letters on the side. It meant nothing to me.

I stared over the trees at the tower blocks. The city was humming but I felt no part of it. It was just like an ant nest. I used to be one of those ants, I thought. But not anymore and I didn't know why. I knew I couldn't last long like this. I'd have to get help somehow.

"Are you right there, mate?" A bloke in a light blue t-shirt and black jeans was standing beside me, holding a tab. The van had stopped near me, with its back doors open.

I glanced up. A blue light flashed and the world went black.

I came around lying on a bed in a cell, like a low budget motel room. As soon as I sat up, a screen on the wall at the end of the bed came to life. A woman's face appeared.

"Welcome to *ProSup*. We want to help. You have been selected for residence because your profile has fallen below critical levels and we can assist you to re-connect. Achieving this may be problematic going forward but with full endeavour, cognitive re-assignment and dedication, you will achieve at least minimum levels and again become a viable and valuable personality.

"First, take up the tab you see beside the bed..."

# SANCTUARY
## Nyssa Baschel

"But I won't be able to breathe," I whispered. The girl with the tail of a fish and soggy hair that clung to her shoulders like seaweed leant closer and I drew back at the pungent stench of salt and ammonia.

"Sure you will," she said. "I'll show you how," and she waved her ivory arm towards the cliff behind me.

I looked up at orange flames licking the treetops, lighting the sky. Wind screamed through branches that leapt off the cliffs only to crash on the jagged rocks below.

"Anyway," her word jolted me back. "You cannot stay here."

I turned towards the moon-drenched water, fighting the sick feeling in my stomach. My throat tightened, making it hard to breathe. She was right; life on land was irreversibly gone.

Anger coursed through me and I clenched my fists. *How had humanity let this happen? The signs had showed for centuries.*

I brushed aside my fringe, hampering my already blurred vision. *Was this it?*

I glanced back at the girl whose glassy eyes were as dark as night. She swayed in the salty water that was my only hope of sanctuary. How could I trust her? She wasn't even human – not anymore, anyway.

*Human*! The word pounded in my head like one of those seismic sledgehammers that tore through hometown last week. Only then did a vague memory wash over me, of a hidden history I had extracted from a broken hydrographic, years ago. Earth was barely recognisable. Not that it mattered now but once it was a given; if you were human you were on top of the evolutionary hierarchy. The greatest threat was other people. Countries were divided until the great collapse of civilisation, something called the Western World fell. I turned and glared at shadows dancing in the flames. I assumed that was the beginning of the end.

Staring back at the fish-girl, she was more than foreign, more than another species. She was female. But what choice did I have?

With a deep breath, I nudged off my blackened runners and, in singed jeans, waded into the waves. They lashed against my thighs before I was ready and I caught my breath to squash a squeal before it escaped my lips. The last thing I wanted was to show her vulnerability. She already knew too much.

Ignoring the hunger playing in her eyes, I stepped out farther, shivering as the icy sea engulfed my waist. Goosebumps broke out on my arms and my teeth began to chatter.

"Are you sure about this?" I whispered.

"Of course." Her voice was too eager. "All you need to do is dream the ocean's depths and want it with all your heart."

I turned to her as a sly smile crossed her face. I stopped and jerked back. *She's lying.*

I spun around and forced my legs through the ocean's rough waters. My hands clutched out at nothing. "No, leave me alone!"

With a powerful thrash of her tail, she leapt out of the waves and caught me around my chest. Her slender arms were slimy as tentacles, and as strong. Her weight knocked me into the sea spray that went up my nose and into my mouth. I plunged forward but she dragged me deeper into the sea. Water swamped me inside and out. Thrashing wildly, the words screamed out in my head – *I'm not ready to die.*

Then her velvety lips enclosed mine. Her breath filled my lungs and an electric pulse coursed through my veins. Seized by convulsions, I was only vaguely conscious of the sharp pain that shot through my spine and into the base of my head. My throat burned and I lost awareness of my legs.

I wasn't sure when I gave up the fight or when everything turned black, but at some point, I glanced up at the moonlight streaming through the hazy water's depth and I surrendered and took my first breath.

The ocean whispered a gentle song at first, but then came the memories that crashed over me like breaking waves. Somehow I understood the chant of an ancient tongue, a warning that had gone unheeded through aeons of seasons that were now abandoning the dance of life.

"*I shall not see a world dear to me,*" the ocean sang in a deep woman's voice with a guttural slur, "*summer without blossoms; cattle will be without milk.*" I thrashed my tail, the currents rushed over my skin. Her words washed through me, singing a truth I had denied. "*Woods without mast, sea without produce—*"

I held arms against my sides as excitement grew from deep inside but my heart was cold. I swam through the murky water immersed in her song, only dimly aware of ruins among the rocks below, worn by centuries of erosion. Rubbish from the upper lands littered the ocean floor. Mangled logos like bitter ghosts of humanity's past, stuck fast on jagged coral.

I couldn't care. The ocean was freedom. Freedom

from being forced to watch the people I loved die from acid rain and sun blisters. Freedom from hunger and scrounging through abandoned cities for shelter from lethally cold nights. Here, in the oceans, nothing mattered.

A rush of bubbles blindsided me and I pivoted around to defend myself.

*"Come with me."* The fish-girl's words echoed in my mind, although her mouth didn't move. Through the fog, I couldn't remember her leaving me or how long I'd been swimming on my own. I swished my tail and propelled myself through shards of sunlight, following her to glowing seagrass and jellyfish. Even the coral, poking over the jagged rocks, radiated deep orange and pink. The girl slowed and waved towards a crevasse with a nod.

*"You want me to go in there?"* I tried to say with my mind. Her blank stare told me I hadn't succeeded and I tried again.

*"You must enter,"* she interrupted. I think she guessed what I was thinking rather than hearing me. *"All women are welcome in Earth's fertile womb."*

*"Women?"* I jerked away from her. *"I'm not a woman."*

Her smile deepened, giving her expression a genuine elegance. *"You are a woman, you couldn't be here if you weren't."*

My mind raced. The idea of being a woman was not only repulsive but downright dangerous. My stomach churned. All I wanted to do was run. The fight for freedom, for the right to breathe free air, for the Androgyny—*had it all been a lie?*

I flinched as she touched my forehead between my eyebrows, spurring a tingling sensation across my face and skull. The ocean brightened. *She* became brighter. I spread out my arms to propel myself backwards but it was too late. The knowledge of the ocean overwhelmed me, hitting me in the solar plexus. I curled to stop myself from vomiting. Ghosts of women, screaming from the brutal abuse of the Breitukaz Precept, reverberated in the core of my being. I knew she spoke the truth, *I am a woman.*

Only then did I let myself fully take in the changes of my body. I made a small groan, it wasn't just the fish-tail. My naked breasts had swollen and my waist had thinned, or was it that my hips beneath the silvery scales were rounder?

The girl ran her fingertips over my cheek as she said, "*You will be accepted here.*" But that brought me little condolence. I didn't want to be the lesser gender, vulnerable to a man's fist with no way to support myself, an inferior birthing machine to the bio-engineering parturition crypts where those of full blood were born.

"*Come,*" she said as I gathered my wits and followed her through a tight gap in the rocks. Seaweed brushed against my skin as I swam towards a blue light beaconing me from the darkness. The water became denser and my fingers and toes tingled but all I could think about was the lie of the life I'd left behind.

I had aspired to win recognition in the Breitukaz Precept despite my androgynous status. Years of bodybuilding and a few forged birth certificates later and I achieved it, until advances in biotesting led to the inquisitions. Then I fled.

Again, the realisation of my womanhood hit me. Had the Androgyny emerged from a faction of desperate women escaping a legacy of oppression? *If only I had access to our history.*

The fish-girl and I emerged into the light and I shadowed her over the steep oceanic trench into the growing darkness that gave way to a brilliant glow. Before me loomed an enormous waterfall sheltering a city nestled deep in the valley of the ocean floor. I squinted through the water; the waterfall had to be an optical illusion, runoff of sand and silt deposits.

"*What is it?*" I forced the question from within my mind.

The girl slowed and swam back towards me. "*It's the fourth great city of the north, Finias,*" she said.

I scanned the urban sprawl of castle towers and dome huts blanketing the aquatic hills before me. In the centre, stone rings surrounded a massive bronze dome emanating shimmering lights. It made no sense, how could this be underwater?

"*Finias?*" I thought.

She smiled. "*We are gifted by the Morrígan, the great phantom Queen, in protection of the feminine. She is the Goddess who blesses those of us fallen in battle who fought for the right to be free.*"

I frowned as the girl turned to swim towards the city and I grabbed her by the arm. My stare demanded the truth. First I discover I'm a woman and the Androgyny is some genetically engineered cover and now this, a race of fish-women blessed by some ancient Deity. The Breitukaz Precept was all I'd ever known, a world of men who owned the weaker sex for their pleasure.

A deep frown crossed her face. "*You must understand, the supremacists will be coming for us.*" Her eyes reached out to me. "*The land wars were only the start.*" I didn't think tears could be seen underwater but she proved me wrong. I think it was the way that her dark irises expanded and how her stare drew me in. "*They will destroy everything,*" she urged, "*every culture – every mother tongue – every memory of humanity.*"

"*But why?*"

She swam up close and whispered with her mind, "*It's not them, it never was.*"

I frowned. *What was she talking about?*

Crinkling her brow, she shook her head as if to say I would never get it then swam away. Her figure became a silhouette in the distant city lights. With a sigh, I trailed behind her down into the bustle of an alien aquatic land.

Cars didn't fly here, nor were they self-contained airtight pods. Instead, they were gold and bronze chariots, pulled through the watery streets by dolphins, creatures that should have been long extinct. Merwomen glided past stone shops with huge windows revealing velvet gowns, intricate jewels – *and shoes.*

I hesitated, but only for a moment so as not to lose my host. Rounding a street corner, I froze. Armed men in oxygen masks, clad in silver armour and tunics, swamped an outdoor assembly. I dove behind a pile of what looked like titanium crates bolted together with thick chains. My mind was focussed on the army. If these men found out I was a woman, I'd be dead.

I looked up to spy the fish-girl peering down at me. A faint smile danced across her face. *"What are you doing?"* she asked.

I looked away and shrugged, hoping she didn't notice my blush.

She glided through the water next to me and whispered, *"Not all men are bad."*

*"But –"*

*"Really. Come, I'll show you."* When she nudged my arm, I refused to budge. She sighed and continued, *"Alright."*

*Finally*, I thought as I straightened to face her, *I might get some sense.*

She frowned. *"The battle-lines are drawn,"* she said. *"Those who stand for freedom and justice will fight this dawn."*

I frowned, she didn't mean the dawn of day as there would be no day, not after the nuclear winter and not underwater.

*"The dawn of humanity. These men were chosen by the Goddess to fight for woman-kind,"* she clarified on cue.

*Of course!* Something deep inside already knew the truth.

She saw that and nodded. *"The one hundred year war ends today,"* she paused, *"and that's why we need you."*

I tensed. *"Me?"*

She nodded again, leaning in close with those night eyes. *"You know them, the Breitukaz Precept, you know their weakness and how to get close."*

I studied her. *"If I knew that, don't you think I would have done something myself?"*

*"No,"* her words echoed in my mind. *"You didn't have what we have. You had no army."*

Then a sensation hit me. It was something so unfamiliar I couldn't work it out.

She smiled and in her mind, she whispered, *"It's called hope."*

Perhaps she was right. Perhaps there was something we could do. Perhaps this race of strangely powerful women could stand up to the Breitukaz Precept. Perhaps there was something to fight for. So I let her lead the way towards the central dome.

Engraved swirls adorned the stone walls as we entered into a pressure chamber. Water filtered out and I found myself standing naked on two very human legs. The girl threw me a shy glance as she too stood fully human and naked until two women entered and swung velvet robes around our shoulders. A million questions ran through my mind but a crashing sound on the other side of the door told me they would have to wait.

"You think you can do whatever you wish with my men," a man's voice roared, breaking the silence I had become accustomed to in a short period of time. His words were not in my head. "I am the Commander."

"You are a man, servant to the Great Queen." A woman's voice echoed through the inner chamber of the dome as we entered. "Question her at your own peril."

My stomach cringed as the man screamed and another crash echoed through the chamber. I looked down at the black marble floor that sent a chill through the souls of my feet. He groaned and I imagined him dragging himself up from the floor to glare at the woman.

"Beg forgiveness," the woman's voice demanded.

He didn't.

A blood-curdling cry filled the chambers, making the hairs on the back of my neck stand on end. I clenched my fists. How was this any different from the Breitukaz Precept?

And then it was silent.

"Stand straight," the girl urged, placing her slender hand on my shoulder. "You're up next."

# GROUND ZERO
## R. A. Purtill

*A tide of scientific research washed up on Alex Frazer's desk one afternoon.*

*It was the sort of afternoon that often came to Alex after a long lunch with long bottles of wine. She blinked and put on her reading glasses before picking up the results that confirmed her worst fears.*

*Together with the usual paperwork, was a phial containing the blood she had requested. This message of plasma in its slim bottle stood on her desk mocking her while she scanned the numbers. Worry formed deep lines across her face.*

"Alex, wake up."

"Wha..?"

"You had another one of your seizures."

Alex groaned and squinted against the sunlight above her. "Oh, Mum, I'm sorry."

"Where were you, darling?"

"In the laboratory after a liquid lunch."

"Drunk? See that's not you at all."

She sat up in the driveway where she had collapsed and massaged her temples. "I saw more this time. The numbers made sense."

"These episodes are scaring me. I think you should see someone."

"No. I'll be all right." She raised herself with a sigh. "I have to go to work." She kissed her mother's cheek and got in the car.

During the drive to the clinic, Alex's mind went back to what she had seen. Her mother was right. With each episode, the visions became clearer but her recovery took longer; even now she forced down lingering nausea. The dizziness stayed, too. Perhaps she shouldn't be driving but she had to get back to the real world as soon as possible. These visions must be put in their place; just her mind playing tricks under the stress of the new job.

She pulled into her car space and grinned. Her car space, her very own, with her name on it: Alex Frazer, Director.

That was it. Those numbers in her vision, they were just numbers, like the statistics she reviewed every day. That's all.

She entered Decontamination. The little cubicle filled with mist and then was vacuumed out and she could see again. Outside her office, a bank of surveillance monitors hung on the wall. One was tuned to television and showed images of the forthcoming launch of the new space mission. She paused there to watch and the handsome new assistant joined her. "Exciting stuff, heh?"

"Yes, you are..." She turned with a smile and then realised her legs were losing strength. Oh. No. Not again. She grasped at the door handle but missed when her knees betrayed her completely.

*If these figures were correct, the phial contained the virus from the Exon V which had crashed on its return from Callisto. A message from outer space had ridden the waves of dark matter to arrive on the shores of Earth. It arrived amongst the flotsam of that doomed mission, delivering its threat to an over-curious monkey before being transferred from the simian's wasted body to the phial now in Alex's hands.*

*And it was that deadly message, in its unassuming bottle, she now carried to Disease Control.*

She focused on the whispering voices around her until the words became intelligible.

"Has there been a recent trauma? A major change in her life? These are the questions we ask after such events."

"A job change, but she was excited about that." Mother's voice was thin and small and she sounded disappointed.

The clinical man continued. "Does anyone in your family show evidence of paranormal abilities? ESP? Clairvoyance?"

"I'm not aware..."

"No psychics? No one who could see into the future?"

"Oh, dear. Now you're scaring me..."

Alex shifted. "Mum?"

"Ah, there you are. I am Doctor Carl."

"I told her I didn't need to see anyone. It's just stress, really." Alex scanned the little man. His head was bald but for the glasses perched there. Under his white lab coat, she could see the collar of a bright Hawaiian shirt. He made notes on his iPad.

"Well, the paramedics didn't think so," said her mother.

"I'm in hospital? No. I can't be. I have to get out..." The action of sitting up pulled at the cannula in her hand. It was connected to a bag of red liquid. Blood? "Is that blood? Get it out of me, get if off." She tugged at the connection and it tore her flesh. She saw the tears in her mother's eyes and observed a silent exchange shared with Doctor Carl.

"You are not in hospital," he said. "You are at the S.E.E.R centre."

Alex scowled at him.

"Scientific Enterprise for Extra-Sensory Research," he announced. "And because of the paranoia you just displayed, you are not going anywhere."

"I am not paranoid." Oh, that sounded paranoid. She paused before slipping on her shoes. "I cannot be here, that's all." She collected her satchel. "I have a life, Mother."

"Be reasonable, darling." Mother touched her arm. "You need help." Alex pulled away.

"You won't be able to leave, Miss Frazer."

"Watch me." Alex exited the room, turned left, decided that was the wrong way, corrected her path and paced down a sterile corridor. It ended in a small recreation room where two people were watching television.

One was a young man dressed in a pale blue shirt and black trousers. His ID hung from a lanyard around his neck. A chaperone for the other, no doubt. The second was a pimply teenager in a green tracksuit. The sort with white binding down the centre of the sleeves and pants, and a wide collar open across the shoulder.

The blue-shirt-guy turned when she arrived and smiled one of those condescending smiles that medical staff have toward the mentally unstable. She hated him for it. The inmate in the bad tracksuit blinked and the image on the television jumped to life with a news report.

"The Exon V will launch today at 10am local time from Cape Canaveral. The latest mission from SpaceX and the Jet Propulsion Laboratory will travel to Callisto, the second moon of Jupiter to bring back..."

Alex grasped the chair near her before her body seized up and the breath left her lungs.

"No. No. It can't be. It can't go." She fumbled through her bag and grabbed her phone. "The news desk now. No, I can't wait, it's urgent. No, don't put me on… damn."

The still smiling orderly was hovering now, too close for her liking. Did he think she would turn violent?

"How do I get out of here?"

He shook his head. "You should go back to your room."

His expectations were met when she grabbed him by the collar with both hands. "Where's the exit?"

Doctor Carl turned up then. "Put Samuel down. Now." Something in his voice made her obey and Samuel restrained her arm, holding it up against her back. She wriggled in his grasp.

"The launch. It can't go ahead. Tell them it can't happen. It ends in disaster. We need to tell them."

"Is it the future you see, do you think?" Doctor Carl was ready to make more notes. She wanted to slap the device from his hands but she refrained and said, "And if it is?"

She wriggled free of Samuel's grasp. He returned to his own patient after a nod from Doctor Carl. The kid jumped from his seat. "Don't let them do any experiments," he called as Samuel herded him out.

"I'm afraid there will be a selection of tests, Alex," said Doctor Carl. "MRI, EEG, bloods. These will determine if your condition is only physical or if indeed you do have prescient ability."

"What about the outcome of the launch?"

"We do not make judgements or intervene. We are only interested in brain science. Hold still."

The sharp and burning sensation in her arm ran through her body and up to her head. Doctor Carl blurred and fuzzed before her eyes, and then all went dark.

*It might have been the bottle from lunch that impaired her thinking that afternoon, or it could have* been the responsibility she bore in the phial of contaminated blood, but Alex Frazer did not see the lights change and so she crossed into the path of a white Camry.

The phial flew in the air, attempting to return its contents to space but the effort was thwarted by Earth's gravity. The container shattered on the pavement and the virus mingled with Alex Frazer's own life source as it leached away.

# SCORPION
# Barry O'Farrell

I have the morning news on to see what's happening with the race to put men on Mars. Of course there's nothing on the topic today. What do I get? Doom and gloom. 'If it bleeds, it leads' as they say in journalistic circles.

A second war with China is brewing; same old dispute, control of the world production of computer chips. Thought the previous war had resolved the matter once and for all. Guess it's been festering quietly in the background. The price of computer chips seems to have stabilised again. A lot of people have been given a bad fright.

Predictably, the next story on the morning news is drug cartel involvement in something or other. It gets repetitious.

I dislike going into the City Morgue. It has an over-sanitised, lingering, biting chemical aroma. Makes my nostrils constrict. The Coroner has called this morning's informal meeting so here I am.

Unsurprisingly, there is a corpse laid out on one of the tables covered with a sheet, except for the feet. I'm guessing this is the cause of today's get together.

I walk over to have a look based on professional and personal curiosity. The big toe of the right foot has the standard ID tag tied to it with string. I read the name. I can't recall seeing the name previously.

"Gil Hart," calls the Coroner by way of recognition as he enters the room. "Hi Seth," I reply as I turn to face him. Seth Goodrich is a tall, thin, cadaverous-looking man who never seems to age. Yes, he looks like his profession. Wonder if he's using the heavily advertised 'Rejuvie' range of products now that that particular scandal has blown over.

"I'd like to introduce you to Kelsi Burke from the Prosecutor's office. Gil is a detective with DNS."

Kelsi is an attractive young lady with long brunette hair. She is dressed conservatively in a dark blue business suit. However, I learnt a long time ago not to judge a book by the model of its Kindle.

I'll bet she is a ferocious opponent in the courtroom, even to those witnesses giving evidence per the ever reliable Li-Fi link. The Courts have phased out Wi-Fi now—like everyone else—though they were among the last to do so.

"Pleased to meet you," says Kelsi as we shake hands. "What is DNS?"

"Dark Net Squad. Don't be surprised if you haven't heard of us. We keep a low profile"

"Of course." Kelsi produces a miniature recording device from her pocket and places it in her right ear. "10 A.M. Meeting with Coroner Seth Goodrich and Detective Gil Hart of DNS..."

"Kelsi," interrupts Seth, "this meeting is informal and preliminary. Put it away."

"Oh, sorry," utters Kelsi and she pockets the earpiece.

"Can you tell me what this is, please?" asks the Coroner holding up an unusual item then passing it to me.

The object in question is a professionally-made piece of work, with three components. A USB connector with a wire coming out of the back end, to which an alligator clip has been affixed.

"Made in China, of course. Customised for single purpose use, nicely made, professionally made. The underworld's new generation have become really good at this hi-tech stuff."

Whilst speaking I discretely manipulate the device. Now with the USB stick lying flat in the palm of my hand, the wire curved back over it and the alligator clip not quite parallel with the stick, I hold out my hand to reveal the profile and say "Scorpion. On the street, they call it a Scorpion. Heard it called other things...Stinger... Link, but mostly Scorpion."

The Coroner raises an eyebrow in my direction so I continue. "The user finds his or her way into a site sourced from the Dark Web. Once logged in and with credits established, the user plugs in the USB, attaches the alligator clip to webbing in between their fingers. The dose is administered."

Kelsi takes a step closer. "What is the drug? How is it administered? Ah, is it a recreational drug?"

"Well," I pause to clear my throat. "Technically there is no drug. It is a series of pulses. Like just about all recreational drugs though, the pulses trigger dopamine neural activity—the pleasure reward. And like all drugs, this is addictive."

"This is confusing. You keep saying drug, dose and then no drug," chimes in Kelsi, "but there is no pharmaceutical?"

"Right."

"As a Prosecutor, what am I to prosecute? We have laws that ban a drug or family of drugs, as—and when—they are identified. In this development, nothing is ingested. Or injected. Or even inhaled. You tell me there is some sort of pulse sent through a computer and down a wire. And let me ask, just how addictive is it? And is this thing lethal?"

"The user sits at their computer. They don't listen to music, dance or party. They sit there stupefied, catatonic like a junkie who has nodded out."

The Coroner walks over to the corpse. "Let me show you something peculiar about this individual." Our host holds up one of the deceased's hands. "Look at the webbing between the fingers."

He draws our attention to a range of little callouses between every finger before highlighting a couple of larger callouses.

He looks to me. "Seems like this person was attached to his computer for long individual sessions over many months. The alligator clip caused callouses to build up, preventing best possible connection. The deceased constantly repositioned the clip trying to achieve maximum effect. Every webbing is affected. I've heard of 'em cutting off fingers but haven't seen any cases yet."

"He must have lived on his computer. What is cause of death?" questions Kelsi.

"He succumbed to a virus," answers Seth knowingly.

"Genus, or type?"

"Computer virus."

# SCHEDULED FOR SERVICE
## Peta Fitzpatrick

### Averil

I pull up in the driveway and James comes screaming towards me. "Why haven't you been answering your phone?"

"What's wrong? What's happened?"

"They've taken Ash."

All I hear now is blood rushing in my ears and my breathing. I never thought it would happen. We listen to the news every night... lots of kids taken by the government under the Advanced State Education Directive but I never imagined it could happen to us. We have evidence confirming we pay for her schooling, the last six years of it...but ...now it hits me, she went to the local state school in year one, before we moved her to the Lutheran school. Only one year! But I thought she was protected, that we'd staved it off through extra fee payments! I don't understand. I taste bile.

There's a flash of black over my eyes as I stumble, my hip hits the car door, but I force myself to stay with it... we have to fix this! There must, *must* be something we can do. They've got this wrong! I'd lain awake nights worrying for my friend Sarah. Her grandson, at a state school, had been taken three months ago. He was only eleven but old enough, the state said, to learn to work, to learn gratitude for a free education. And I'd thanked the universe that we had been safe... I thought we were safe.

Our boys, Perry and Gray, were never in danger. Five and ten years older than their sister, they'd gone through school before the Directive became a reality but my baby girl was in the system after the retrospective cut-off. We were always aware how lucky we were to have scored a place at private school before the Directive was announced. Parents fought each other for places outside the state system, queuing for hours, overnight, with police brought in to manage the panicked.

We knew that Ash would have to 'Serve'—as they call it—for some of her teenage years, as the funded portion of her Lutheran education was repaid, but it wasn't time... not yet... They'd told us her first year of school was exempt from triggering early service, that it would be added on to the end, that she wouldn't start before seventeen, could finish her schooling...we have the papers... I can't understand it.

I focus on James' face... it looks strange, blurred round the edges... only seconds have gone by and he is telling me how it happened, monotone. "They knocked, they entered, she was doing her homework, and they took her, took our daughter. She kept saying 'no'. Not screaming it, not even raising her voice. Just a quiet 'no, no' over and over and over." At that, James' voice cracks and he crumples to the grass, taking me with him. Against his chest, I start with a rush of "But, but they've got it wrong. We can fix this." I lift my head and scour his face. "What did they say to you when they came? Did they give you any papers? Oh god, my baby, she's only thirteen."

I drag myself up and partly haul James to his feet. By the time I make it inside, the boys burst through the front door, calling for us. They know she's gone, someone told them, maybe Mel, I don't know. Gray strides over and clutches my arm. Perry backs up against the wall and slams both fists backwards on either side of him. James staggers in and leans over the kitchen table, heaving. I pick up the phone with a trembling hand.

Ash

I'm the only one on the bus, the only kid. Thing 1 and Thing 2 are both up front. I can't see shit through the windows. They're mostly covered with posters about 'The Privilege of Service' and the 'Benefit to Society of the Adolescent Training and Workforce Preparation Act'. I might not be quite thirteen yet, but I'm not stupid. This is about making money. Anyone can tell you that. Back when the government 'lost the plot' as Gray puts it, they also lost any cred when they first tried to pretend this was an idea to benefit us kids. Their stupid posters say things like to 'reduce the burden on families during those difficult teenage years' and 'give our young people a sense of hope and direction' and 'prepare tomorrow's adults for innovative workforce initiatives'. And they pay someone to sit and come up with this crap? They'd use any excuse now to wring what they can out of people.

I lean forward, pushing my forehead against the green vinyl of the seat in front of me. Mum and Dad will sort this out. I know they will. I need to pee. All that they said when they took me was that I had been 'identified for processing'. And they never looked me in the eye. Not once. They know this is a shitty thing to do to a kid. And they made me leave my phone behind. I was on the bus before Dad even realised what was happening. But I knew. Everyone knows there's no talking it over. A girl a grade above me got taken the same way from school yesterday while we all watched. When I get home, I'm gonna slam them so hard it'll go viral in milliseconds! I've really gotta pee. Teesh won't know what's happened, I said I'd ring her after she'd finished netball. Feeling pretty shit-scared actually.   But I won't be able to stop laughing when they've gotta turn this bus around.

## Averil

I've been on the phone for two hours. The Workforce Preparation Department office closes at five and I have to start again. They transfer me to the after-hours 'Parent Information Line', which is giving me no bloody information whatsoever. I'm on hold and on my second cup of cold tea – Perry keeps making tea, his mother's son. The same recurring minute of Mozart drills into my ear, spoiling him forever. I print a wet pattern on the table with the rings left by my cup. James has gone next door to see if Melinda saw any other activity in the street before they came to our house. Gray is on the computer, next to me, checking in with his mob, looking for any underground news. His theory is there's been another policy change and they've stuffed the notifications up again. But I can't think that way. It's just a mistake. A mix-up, a giant unbelievable cockup. They're going to realise and she'll be home by bedtime, I feel it.

## Ash

The bus is stopping. If we're not there yet, I can maybe use someone's phone. I can at least find a toilet. The door opens and I step down onto gravel. Thing 1 jumps down from the front cabin, slams the door and bangs on it twice. Thing 2 swings the bus away from us, into a large shed and out of sight. Thing 1 says, "Come," and I follow him down a cement ramp to a huge glass door. He punches numbers into a keypad and the door pivots open with a hiss, then we're inside.

It's not ordinary quiet so much as like a funeral home. There's something like a slow, sad murmur coming out of the walls, the floor. I can't really hear anyone. But they're here. I don't need to pee anymore. I feel strange. Like I'm seizing up into a glacier. It's cold. I'm cold. And going numb. "Follow," says Thing. Down another ramp, along a bare corridor and I am in a room. Not much bigger than the bed inside it, no windows, no anything, no explanation. "Why am I here?" I plead with Thing 1, my voice sounds like I'm about six. As he pulls the door closed he murmurs, "You've been scheduled for Service."

## Averil

I've been crying enough to make focusing on the screen a bitch. Yesterday's reply from the WP tells me nothing. A name, a birthdate, the words 'Identified for processing 23rd January 2026. Scheduled to commence Service 26th January 2026'. But it's my baby's name, her birthdate, and she's gone. They won't tell us where she is, only that they will confirm her work plan with us by the end of the week. They won't let us talk to her until 'she's settled'. I am terrified. And sick. I never thought this could happen to us. We had clear confirmation.

Since the directive came in three years ago, the birth rates have already started dropping a little. I get it. I so get it. People feeling too scared to have children. There's a lot of furious talk about the directive, and constant protests calling for the system to be scrapped. The opposition is well aware that this is leverage for them, and soon they will use it to get into power and this nightmare will be over. It may, hopefully, only be a reality for a few years, but there are still thousands of kids who've been caught up in this. And families minus a child or two.

My computer pings, a message has arrived. We know where she is.

### Ash

There's twelve of us here, I think. Newbies. You aren't here for long before you get 'placed' somewhere. Rosie, the kid opposite me at breakfast, says six kids got moved out yesterday, and they'd been there for three days. She's been here for two, so I suppose she'll go tomorrow and I won't be far behind. Unless Mum and Dad get me out of here first. Rosie shakes her head at this and tells me about one of the last lot who kept saying the same thing, very loudly, and only got laughed at by Thing 1 and Thing 2. Seems, between them, they're about it for this place.

Last night I curled up in the dark, crying for Mum and pleading with Logic to fix this, but Logic wasn't listening. This morning, I am going to be patient. I can't do anything in here. Tears are useless—they won't stop anyway, so I ignore them. But when I get moved, then I can surely talk to Somebody In Charge, explain there's been a mistake, ask them to ring my parents, to check, to take me home.

### Averil

Ash has been gone for three days. James and I haven't gone to work, have hardly slept. The boys aren't home, trying to find out anything they can to help their sister. I never knew I had so many tears in me, or so much anger. The phone rings. A woman with a cardboard voice tells us Ash is being moved to the Petrie Training Campus today. James grabs the car keys. I ask her to explain why this is happening, but she's apparently only authorised to give me Ash's transfer information. Bullshit. I demand to speak to her superior. The phone goes dead.

"I'll drive," says James. He sounds relieved to have an action he can take. We know where the campus is, we'd driven there with Sarah when she wanted to see her grandson, Luca, but they wouldn't let her in, as she wasn't the parent. Now, this gives me hope for us. On the drive there, I get back on the phone. *"The wait time on the Parent Information Line is approximately 50 minutes. You are progressing in the queue".* We'll be at the Petrie campus in half that time, but I stay on the phone, useless, too scared to hang up. I want my baby girl back with me. I retch and swallow. The world slides past my window. We pass Woolworths. People are putting groceries in their cars. A man puts petrol in his four wheel drive and yells at his kids through the window. A woman walks two dogs, their leads tangled around each other. *"The wait time on the Parent Information Line is approximately 45 minutes. You are progressing in the queue".*

Ash

I'm back on the bus this morning. Rosie is with me, and five others, not counting Thing 1, and Thing 3 who mysteriously appeared this morning. Obviously, there's more of them running the show, and we have *no* idea of what's going on here. Thing 1 has told us we're going to the Petrie Training Campus. There was no pretend joy in his voice, he's clearly aware it's pointless, as we're not stupid enough to believe this is like some camp we're going on. "It's good we're going there," I tell Rosie, "I live pretty close to it. It'd be worse if we were further away. My parents will sort this out." Poor Rosie lives miles from there, she hasn't heard from her parents either. I'm sure mine can help her, too.

I recognise where we are, and sit up, ready. They've changed the roads a bit and there are new lights, turning red. We come to a stop next to a sign with a sickening picture of happy teenagers in a workshop, laughing over a benchtop strewn with tools. I miss the words as the lights change and we pass more signs; kids at work in a computer lab that looks like a Google wonderland, smiling kids in a brightly-lit factory, kids running around a track, looking ecstatic to be doing laps, getting fit... The visual torture ends as the bus turns into a large parking area, fences and more fences ahead. Maybe twenty cars parked. We stop and Thing 1 gets up as a woman comes out of a booth before the gate.

I jump as I hear a loud bang on the side of the bus. Then my name, "Ash, Ash!" Another bang. My dad is running alongside the bus, jumping, hitting the bus, looking for me. I stand up and scream "Here! I'm here. Dad! Daddy!" He sees me and starts yelling but so does Thing 1 and I miss what Dad says. Thing 1 is yelling at him to get away from the bus. I see Mum running towards us, she drops her phone, doesn't stop. She's crying as she runs, calling my name. Everything is happening. Rosie grabs my shoulders, yelling, "We're here!" Thing 3 barks at us to sit down. I hammer on the glass. Dad's fingertips reach the bottom of the window, Mum doesn't even come close, she backs up so she can see me. She looks straight at me, desperate, terrified. I feel more scared than I've ever felt, seeing the dread in her eyes. The bus jolts and we pull towards the gates. Dad keeps hitting the side of the bus, they're running. I hear them both screaming my name, then there's a second when I realise we've been severed... they're behind us. We're through the gates. Mum and Dad are getting fainter until I can't hear them. The bus pulls around a huge red brick building and then I can't see them anymore. Thing 1 and Thing 3 are muttering to each other, shaking heads, shrugging shoulders. This obviously isn't new to them.

Rosie and I hold hands. The bus stops.

# HALF A FLAMING INCH
## Rollo Waite

Golden sand, gently rolling surf, Sunshine Coast paradise— Kawana Beach stretching nine kilometres, Caloundra to Mooloolaba—where Greg and Rita Molloy built their family home, near the beachfront in 1995. They were young and athletic. They could surf just a stone's throw from home. If Greg wanted, there was Point Cartwright, where he could ride his board off the rocks. He loved surf fishing—could walk to the top of the dunes and expertly spot the schools of fish that moved along the coast and catch a feed before they were netted. This was their Eden.

When they first planned to move there, Greg's dad, Eric, berated his son. "Greg, you're bloody mad building so close to the ocean."

"Why's that?"

"Fact is you're about half a flaming inch above sea level. If there's ever a surge in the sea, you're stuffed."

"What do you mean a surge in the sea?"

"A tsunami."

"But Dad, they're in other places. Japan. The Philippines."

"Son, you can have them anywhere, just needs an earthquake off the coast and you're in big... trouble."

"Can also get run over by a bus. I might be only half an inch above sea level, but that's all good."

Eric went on. "And there's this climate change stuff—global warming, El Niño... Have you considered that?"

"I reckon that's mostly a heap of bullshit put out by those boffins, like that joker you know at UQ—what's his name?"

"Alex Sazonov."

"Yeah, and those others in the CSIRO—nothing better to do with their time than stuff around doing Mickey Mouse, modelling stuff. It's garbage."

"OK be an ignoramus, but don't insult Alex Sazonov—he's the greatest climatologist in the world. Just remember, smart arse... I warned you."

But Greg remained unconvinced and they settled into and worked on the Sunshine Coast. They surfed, they fished and continued old ties with their lifesaver friends from their single days. Then their family arrived and slowed them down. But they thrived.

Summer 2016 was hot and exceptionally dry. "More climate change," Greg grudgingly admitted to his father. His scepticism was becoming watered down. After years of drought until 2010, huge areas of Queensland were set awash with the highest rainfall ever recorded. Then followed the great Brisbane floods of 2011, when the city was brought within inches of being washed away by the raging waters and the Wivenhoe Dam almost burst. If that wasn't enough, there were the disastrous Australia Day floods of 2013, where Bundaberg, Gympie, Mundubbera and other places were almost destroyed by record flooding.

Greg's Sunshine Coast survived this—just. There was extensive damage on the beachfront at Maroochydore, Mooloolaba and Noosa. As he viewed the grim footage on television, his father's words came back to haunt him; 'Half a flaming inch above sea level.' It wasn't a tsunami that worried him, but the tidal surges that increasingly devastated the

beaches and the dunes with wind and water—
already happening all along the coast.

Australia Day, 2017—in the academic solitude of his
climate simulation laboratory, University of
Queensland, a studious man in his late thirties was
hunched over one of a network of computers. On the
screens were arrays of hieroglyphics—rolling,
interacting over Landsat imagery—like a cosmic
computer game, but deadly serious. Alexander
Nikolayevich Sazonov was on the job night and day,
engaged in something that only he understood. This
unpretentious son of a Russian immigrant from
Brisbane's West End was regarded as a genius—
some even said 'Another Einstein'. In the ivory
towers of climatology, he was fast becoming the
world's most highly-acclaimed modeller of climate
change. He had his critics in academia—those who
called him an idiot or *prophet of doom*—who had
neither the brains nor the wit to appreciate his
concepts but purported to know all the mysteries of
the universe.

Through his modelling, Alex had predicted the
calamitous droughts and floods in Australia in the
21st Century. But no one believed him until after the
event, and some said he had just been lucky. Nothing
fazed Alex. His maxim: *Facts not words*.

Eric Molloy lived next door to Alex in St Lucia.
They sometimes got together on Friday evenings for
a chat and a few beers. Alex lived a somewhat
cloistered life, often with little company other than
the faces of computers, seething with symbols,
responding to the algorithms he fed into them.

"I must simply get it as right as I can, despite
fluctuating patterns," Alex said one evening. "Your
son at Buddina will certainly be in big trouble if the
current trends continue. There seems to be a gradual

progression towards dislocation of the El Nino/La Nina phenomenon. That's bad enough in the long term. What really worries me is the potential melting of the polar ice caps that I'm modelling. Just imagine the amount of water that would flow into the sea if they completely melted. I believe Noah's flood would be on again if there was a total thaw."

Eric choked on his beer and his voice quivered. "Shit! Even a partial thaw would be bad enough. Do you know, even Greg is getting a bit twitchy now. And I don't think he's heard about the polar caps—just worries about all the bad weather. Bloody hell, half an inch above sea level—not much hey? And goodbye to civilisation as we know it if there is a complete meltdown. "

Alex smiled reassuringly. "I really don't think that will happen—at least not for a few thousand years. No, it's this bloody Pine Island Glacier, in Antarctica that's the worry. It developed a giant crack, October 2011. By May 2012, satellite images showed a second crack and a giant iceberg broke away—720 square kilometres—the size of the city of Chicago. That's only the South Pole. The Arctic sea ice, February 2014, was 910,000 square kilometres below the 1981-2010 average. All of this is quite a worry. I've been modelling the undermining and melting down of both polar ice caps. Look, I can't say much more as I'm bound by certain official protocols. However, tell Greg, if I was him, I'd be moving to higher ground by 2024."

News about the polar caps sent shivers up Greg's spine. "This climate change is bad enough, but the polar caps—the last bloody straw. We're getting out, Rita—the sooner the better."

She couldn't believe her ears. "I thought you said that this climate change stuff was bullshit?"

"I've changed my mind, love. This Alex joker, next door to Dad, he's a world authority. Reckons we ought to get out while the going is good, by 2024."

By Easter 2022 the Molloys moved from Buddina to the heights of Mapleton. They missed the beach and being half an inch above sea level and all the rest—but they felt safe.

Christmas Eve, 2022: Alex burst in on Eric with a stack of food, bottles of champagne—grinning from ear to ear.

Eric couldn't believe it. He'd only seen the serious, thoughtful Alex, but this guy was looking for a party. "Eric, you won't believe it, but the whole bloody thing has turned around."

"What do you mean?"

"Irrefutable evidence that the polar meltdown has been reversed. I haven't told anyone, but I've been modelling the frequency and intensity of sunspots of data collected over the past hundred years, as accurately as I can."

"Yeah, so what?"

"They're positively associated with the status of the polar ice caps—high activity, increased melting—low activity, aggregation of ice, even another ice age—but millions of years away. Sunspot activity is in the process of gradual recession. And, by the way, this means the degree of climate change is most likely receding. My modelling shows reversion. So all those critical bastards won't be able to call me the *prophet of doom* anymore. I'll bloody well show them!" Alex noted the shock on his friend's face. "Eric, aren't you glad? Isn't this about the best news you've ever heard? Oddly enough the climate change sceptics were right but didn't know why. Before I forget, you should tell Greg that he doesn't need to move now."

"Sorry Alex, but it's too late. He's up at Mapleton."

"Oh, shit, Eric, I'm sorry, but I *did* specify exactly 2024."

# WHO'S WHO
## J. H. Nelson

Handing Ruby her lunch, I notice the ant-like drawing and wonder what it is. I sit with her and we eat together.

"What is your drawing of, sweetie?"

"The bad men coming. Here is our house. This is Aki's house. See, Mummy?" As her stubby finger points, I see the picture through new eyes. It is an alarmingly accurate map of our neighbourhood. The 'bad men' are the swarm of ants I saw.

"What is this over here?" I question of a circular scribble.

"That is this man's. He's burning." She eats her sandwich, unfazed by my questions.

"What do you mean he is burning, honey? He can't hold fire, fire burns our skin. Or is he a magic man?" I smile. Maybe I've read too much into it.

"No, he carries it on top of his stick. You know, like Grandpa has at the pool!"

I dig around in the archives of my brain, trying to work out what she is talking about and think of anything she has seen or heard that could have inspired such a story. I excuse her from the table and she toddles off to play. Getting back to my housework, I can't shake the uneasy feeling that it is happening again.

Buckling her into the car, we talk about picking up her daddy and what we will make for dinner—a conversation that continues as we drive off, down the road.

"That's bad man's house. They'll come from in there." Ruby's shift back to the bad man story makes the hairs on the back of my neck stand up. I make a mental note of the house from the corner of my eye but carry on our original discussion, feigning ignorance.

Ruby is finally down for the night. Derek and I sit down together to eat dinner, something we rarely achieve these days.

"Ruby drew a picture today," I say, handing him the illustration.

"Hm, looks great. Can you pass the salt, please?" He shows little interest towards the paper, waiting for the salt shaker.

"I think it might be another one of *those* drawings, Derek. She tells me that these are bad guys and this is our house here. This is Amani and Rafiq's place, here. And this..." I point to the circular scribble, "is this man's fire torch! And then, later when we came to pick you up this afternoon, she says to me out of nowhere—you know that cottage up on the corner, the one with the pristine lawn and the old guy who's out there every day primping it?—that is where the bad man lives. She said that is where they'd come from!" My finger jumps madly all over the page as I revisit all the elements that Ruby explained earlier.

"Don't be ridiculous, Sam! She probably just saw something on TV and has put together this long-winded fairytale. You're reading too much into it." His fork hits the edge of his plate with a loud clunk, splattering gravy onto the cream tablecloth. I rise to get a damp cloth before it stains.

"I can't believe you are going to deny this! You did that last time and it cost lives! How can you honestly sit there and delude yourself that her drawings are nothing more than just the imagination of a child?" Returning with the cloth, I scrub at the linen with more force than is necessary.

"Because we're talking about the scribbles of a three-year-old! Toddler artwork is for fridge doors, it isn't supposed to be scrutinised by bored mothers who should perhaps leave the house a little more frequently."

"Why do you ignore this? Why do you never believe her? Despite the fact that she keeps proving herself right!"

"That warehouse delivery was a coincidence! There is no way she could have known what it held inside!"

"That is exactly my point, Derek. She does know! And I suppose the man beside us at the traffic lights that day was just a coincidence too!?!"

"She was a *baby*, Samantha. *Yes*, I think it was a coincidence!"

"She said bye-bye and we both know it." Plate in hand, I leave him and go to load the dishwasher. I am still stacking the last of the cooking utensils when Derek arrives with his empty plate. Leaving it on the sink, he turns to leave in silence.

"If you think I will just sit back and watch again as more lives are put in danger—danger that we might be able to stop—you are very wrong!"

"You sound like a lunatic, and worse, you're turning our daughter into a freak show! Just remember she has to live with this."

These are the last words spoken between us that night.

Preparing for a disaster with only some of the information quickly proves to be harder than I could have imagined. *What will spark this 'bad man' army?*

*Who or what are they after? What will the victims be trying to shield against? Who is going to be the target?*

"Why are the bad men in our street, Ruby? Do you know who they are looking for?" I plead with her to tell me everything she knows but naturally, she chooses today to revert back into a none-the-wiser child, leaving me to question if I am indeed mad and dreamt the whole thing up. I continue to probe her gently with questions throughout the day, to no avail. Knowing that her first premonition came only seconds before impact, I panic about the time frame.

We had been on our way to a festival when a drunk driver ran the red light and careened into the car beside us, killing its driver instantly. The most recent of her visions had come with a little more notice. She had told me a vivid tale of someone putting fire in the mail, in the car on our way to daycare. On our way home that afternoon, we heard on the radio a mirrored version—a local business had accepted a bomb disguised as a parcel. In a warehouse full of highly flammable goods, the poor souls hadn't stood a chance of escaping.

I walk into the street, glancing up and down, looking for a sign—anything—to hint at the answers that would bring all the missing pieces together. Nothing! I check the letterbox with a heavy heart; I'm not going to be able to stop it, I can feel it in my bones. Amani, my neighbour and friend across the road, pulls into her driveway and we wave to one another. Ruby sees the car from the front door and takes off after them at a run.

"Aki, Aki!" she squeals. I manage to catch her before she runs across the street. On my hip, we cross to say hello. Safely on the other side, I put Ruby down to play.

"Hi, Akilah, how was kindy today? Hi, Amani."

"Hi! Hi, Ruby, how are you, sweetheart?" Amani

lifts Akilah down and out of the car. The two girls scamper off to dig for worms in a pot plant by Amani's front door.

"How are things with Rafiq's work? Have they settled down?"

"Not really. Another three were let go last week and they're threatening more before next pay day. Rafiq is looking elsewhere but everyone wants a profile photo so he isn't getting any calls. If he loses this job, I'm afraid we'll have to move into the safe-house community farther west." Tears rim Amani's eyes.

"There is nothing safe about those communities." Everyone knew the stories of crime, rape and murder that were all too frequent amongst those who lived there.

"Yes, and I fear it is a one-way ticket to Tennant Creek Concentration Camp. It is suicide." Amani clutches her face in her hands and begins to weep.

As emotion engulfs us both and I hold her clinging form, fear and understanding meld together, making my brain work faster and clearer. *This is it! This is what they are coming for—to force Amani's family from their home and out of our neighbourhood!*

"Amani, listen to me!" I stare at her with desperation. "There is a mob and I think they're coming for you! It will be soon and you must do as I tell you, now! They will be on foot and they'll march from up that side of the street, and they are dangerous! When I say, get in your car and leave as if your and Akilah's life depend on it! Now, go and pack some clothes for you and Akilah. Nothing definitive. You'll need to carry Akilah so keep your hands free." I shove Amani towards her front door as I speak, my plan forming with every step.

"Sam, I don't understand... what are you...?"

"There is no time to explain, Amani. Please just do

as I say and trust me. You need to get away from here and not come back to my house or yours. I don't know if you will *ever* be able to come back, you need to understand the severity, please! I will text you our next move. I need to figure out somewhere safe. I'm going to find a way to hide you, Amani, I will do everything I can to keep you girls safe until all this is over. Do you understand?"

Amani stares at me, confused and concerned about my mental well-being, I'm sure. But I have got through to somewhere deeper in her soul, she is listening and heeding my warning.

"Rafiq?" Amani whispers.

"I think it will be safer for you and Akilah if you leave without him. I'm so sorry. We'll see what happens. I need to get back and make plans of my own. We will need food; if you have any tins, put them in a box, I will be back soon to pick them up. Now go!" Amani scurries inside. I scoop Ruby into my arms and send Akilah in behind her mother.

Time passes quickly but I have sorted bedding, toiletries, nappies and a bunch of extra stuff I think we might need. *Time is our enemy, if only I knew when!* With nothing left to pack, I go to raid Amani's kitchen.

Mess is everywhere. Clothes are strewn all over the lounge room with an up-ended laundry basket next to the dining table. We work in strained silence together. Amani tries to pack her whole life into a bag while I load fridge and pantry goods into an old storage tub I found in her garage. I try to keep it to the basics, but things like fruit and perishables can be used first. I load as much as I can fit and carry into the container. I leave Amani and struggle with the box towards my own front door.

The neighbourhood stickybeak, Mrs Kinnley, walks by me at the edge of the road, greeting as she passes. I nod and smile as she continues up the street. I glance at her some seconds later and our eyes meet. She gives me an evil smirk before turning away. *She knows!* Beyond her, multiple cars gather, coming into sharp focus at the far end of the road. *Dear God*! Food litters my lawn as I drop the container and run for Amani's front door, screaming.

"Now, Amani! You must go! Take your phone! Put Akilah in the car and go! Now! Now!" I am banging on the front door when her car squeals out of the garage.

I race home and scour the lawn for produce and cans. Filling my arms multiple times, I dump them inside my front door until everything is gone. Finding Ruby building a tower with the canned vegetables on the kitchen floor, I leave her playing, lock the screen door and text Amani.

"Don't come home. Just keep driving. I will call ASAP."

Noise builds outside. Terror grips me. *Have I done the right thing? What if I am wrong and it's us who are not safe? I should've taken Ruby away from here! Now it is too late to leave.*

Louder still, the rioters move into my line of vision. Soundlessly, I close the front timber door for added protection and slip into the study where I can see and not be seen.

The world as I know it slips from its axis. There, among the cultural enforcers, I stare straight into the eyes of...

*Derek?*

# THE TRAVELLER
## Matthew J. Hellscream

Maximillian Mortimer looked over the placement of the food on his dining room table. He had agonised over the food choices for months. A vast array of fresh fruits from across the globe had been flown in to create an incredible fruit platter. Pedestrian items like apples, grapes and bananas were interspersed with more rare, unique specimens such as the chocolate-like cupuaçu, grilled jackfruit, and sliced starfruit.

Another platter was piled with pastries. Croissants, doughnuts, cronuts, brioche rolls, and more. Nearby was an array of different types of chocolates. White chocolate dipped raspberries, bitter dark chocolate buttons, and a variety of 21st-century chocolate bars.

An assortment of meats had been arranged at the end of the table. A basket of southern fried chicken sat next to a platter of barbequed meat. Sausage links, char-grilled sirloin steak, slow-cooked pulled pork and lamb cutlets. Then there was a tray heaped with racks of pork ribs, with necessary napkins.

Maximillian's chefs had outdone themselves.

In the centre of the table were three pots of brewed coffee. Coffee, it was said, was the crowning achievement of human civilisation. How sad a future it would be if coffee no longer existed.

Maximillian had no idea how many people would

show up for his party. No-one would know about its existence until three days from now. The advertising was extensive and had been incredibly expensive. An entire media blitz would occur. Of his billions of dollars, this experiment had cost Maximillian a few paltry million. He wouldn't miss it, even if the experiment failed.

He glanced at his watch. Ten minutes until the party was due to start. The party that no-one knew about. His aim was to prove whether time travel was possible. As one of the planet's most influential people, he was sure that he would go down in the history books as someone of importance. A hero.

Maximillian made his fortune in the early Dot-Com boom, and before that bubble burst, he'd invested in the future of humanity; clean energy research firms and sustainable farming technology. With the world's population set to explode during his lifetime, there were three things that would always be necessary: Energy, food and water.

His investments were not always altruistic. Some avenues of research would not bring financial returns. Their societal impacts were unquestionable, but they would never make money. So, he financed up and coming companies who promised to be profitable, purely to funnel those profits into other projects, which were working for the good of humankind. For the future of planet Earth.

Maximillian didn't like the composition of how the meat looked on the table. He moved the fried chicken closer to the racks of pork ribs, then moved the tray of barbequed meats more to the side, so it lay perpendicular to ribs. He glanced at his watch again.

It was eleven o'clock, and the time had arrived.

If time travellers existed, surely, they would be punctual. Maximillian watched the minutes tick by. With each passing second, his mood darkened. The money he'd already paid for the advertising was non-refundable. He abhorred waste.

Eleven o'clock came and went. Maximillian poured himself a coffee, scooped two teaspoons of sugar into it, then stirred. He pulled out a chair and sat, his back to the front door. He drank the entire cup in four long swallows.

Then came the knock. Time seemed to dilate as those sharp taps echoed through the entryway. Maximillian became acutely aware of the quickening pace of his heart. The skin on the back of his neck prickled. The guests were late, but he had been right!

Time travel was possible.

Maximillian straightened his tie, royal purple against the black shirt beneath. He strode towards the front door, grasped the handle, and opened it.

The man that stood before him did not quite appear as Maximillian had expected. He looked to be in his early twenties. He was tall, and fit, with a short black beard. His long hair was tied back in a ponytail. He wore a simple black t-shirt and dirty, frayed blue jeans, cinched at his waist with a battered leather belt. He wore a watch on his left wrist; a simple timepiece that appeared to have originated in this time period, with a cracked face.

Maximillian deflated.

"Can I help you?" he asked.

"Am I late for the party?" the man asked with a wry smile.

"I'd say you're just on time," Maximillian replied, grinning.

Maximillian led the time traveller into the dining room. There were so many questions he wanted to ask, but there was one that burned hotter than the others.

"So, are there any more of you coming?" Maximillian asked.

"Just me, I'm afraid."

"That's a tad disappointing. May I ask why?"

"This party goes down in the history books as a complete and utter failure. No-one shows up, aside from me, a homeless young man searching for his next meal. Because your party is a bust, and someone shows up to your door anyway, you decide to feed him. Don't worry, the story goes very well for you. It really does help with your good-guy image."

The traveller turned away from the food and spread his hands out in front of him, as though displaying a banner.

"Do-gooder billionaire feeds the homeless after his time travel experiment fails spectacularly."

The traveller turned back towards the table and inspected the food on offer. He chuckled to himself.

"What's so funny?" Maximillian asked.

"We still have fruit in the future, you know. And we still eat meat. We got the whole galaxy hooked on coffee, too."

"The whole galaxy?" Maximillian asked. The ramifications of that simple, off-hand comment made his head swim.

The traveller turned back towards Maximillian. "Sit down before you fall down."

Maximillian walked towards the table, pulled a chair out, and almost fell into it. The traveller walked around the table, smiling quietly to himself as he heaped his plate with food. He poured two cups of brewed coffee.

"Cream and sugar?" the traveller asked.

"Black and two."

The traveller obliged, then passed the coffee across the table.

Maximillian took it and watched the traveller closely as he popped a grape into his mouth and chewed.

"I bet you were thinking that in the future, we all subsist on various kinds of protein bars. Everything made out of beans and shit, right?" the traveller asked.

"I didn't know. I made some assumptions," Maximillian admitted.

"I'll admit that most people from my time live on meat alternatives. We grow meat instead of harvest it from animals. No brain. No consciousness. No pointless killing required."

"And fruit?"

"We still have fruit. Lots more varieties, though."

"From other planets?" Maximillian hazarded a guess.

The traveller smiled, neither confirming nor denying the implications of Maximillian's question.

"So, what, you can't actually tell me?"

The traveller laughed, loud and unrestrained. "I can tell you..."

"But you'd have to kill me?" Maximillian asked.

"No, it's just too much fun messing with you," the traveller admitted.

"You shit!" Maximillian said, incredulous. Despite himself, he laughed.

"I'm not here for pleasantries, though. We have a lot to discuss," the traveller said.

"Of course."

"First thing's first; regardless of how you feel at the end of this, you need to ensure that your advertising goes ahead. You are to do every interview that is requested of you, and in each of those interviews you are to express your frustration that the only person who showed up was a homeless youth, who you elected to share your food with."

Maximillian nodded.

"People don't want the truth, Max. I can call you Max, right?"

Maximillian shrugged. He didn't care one way or the other.

"The truth has a habit of terrifying people. The world isn't ready for the knowledge that time travel is possible. Hell, the future I'm from isn't even ready for it to be general knowledge."

"Where are you from, exactly?"

"Where, or when?"

"Both, I guess," Maximillian said.

"I'm from the Agency," the traveller said.

"Which agency?"

"*The* Agency," the traveller replied, as though the emphasis communicated a deeper meaning that Maximillian should recognise.

"I don't follow."

"That's fine. Let me ask you a question. Where do you see the human race ending up in the next five hundred years?"

Maximillian paused to consider the question. "I want to see humanity band together. I want to see the end to bloodshed over resources, and over-competing political and religious ideologies. I want humanity to be united and at peace."

"I didn't ask you what you wanted," the traveller said. "I asked where you *saw* humanity ending up."

Maximillian exhaled through his nose. "If we keep polluting our planet the way we are, we won't just kill all the other species that call it home, but we'll destroy ourselves. If we keep fighting and dying over money, there is no happy ending."

"But it's necessary," the traveller said.

Shocked, Maximillian's jaw dropped. "What the hell do you mean?"

"People don't thrive in peace," the traveller said. "They don't make technological leaps and bounds when their families are safe and sound at home. Not when they have all the time in the world. Humanity thrives under pressure. It is when we are cornered that we are our most powerful, our most imaginative, and our most inventive."

"What are you trying to say?"

"It's our destiny to destroy this planet. Everything you have spent your life dedicated to up until this point hasn't been a waste, though. Clean energy is a worthwhile pursuit, but the destruction of our Genesis planet is necessary. When faced with our own extinction, it is the fuel that burns away in the heart of humanity that gives us the push to do the things we need to do to join the galactic community. We just need you to refocus your resources."

Maximillian stared into the black depths of the coffee cradled in his hands. This planet, the birthplace of humanity, was destined to be destroyed? No. It couldn't be. He'd spent his life investing in technologies that could help people and repair the damage done to this planet.

He glanced up at the traveller, who was studying Maximillian's face intently.

"You don't believe me," the traveller said.

"I don't know what I believe. How can the destruction of a planet be necessary?"

The traveller withdrew a device from his pocket and set it on the table. It looked like an ordinary cell phone, albeit a nondescript brand. The display lit up, then projected an image of a slowly rotating galaxy above the surface of the table.

The traveller touched the display, which reacted to his touch as though it had a physical presence.

"This is where Earth currently is. This outer spiral arm, here," the traveller said. The display zoomed into a planet covered in storms. Small sections of blue and brown appeared between the clouds, but they were few and far between. The planet was smothered. "Our new homes are spread across the

Milky Way Galaxy."

The traveller zoomed out of the display and highlighted three planets. They had names. The first was called New Earth. The second, Central, and the third, Orpheon.

"New Earth?" Maximillian asked.

"That's it. That's home," the traveller said. "Over 23 billion humans live on New Earth, and it truly is a paradise. We've learned from our mistakes, and the renewable energy tech developed by Mortimer Industries is what allows us to get there. Then, once we're there, it lets us survive and thrive. You might be tempted to pull the plug on your arc reactor project. I believe it has stalled for the last few years?"

"It has," Maximillian admitted. No-one external to the project was supposed to know any of the details.

"There will come a time soon when the pieces will all fit together. Don't despair. Keep funding the project, even when it feels like you're just throwing your money into a black hole. But there is one thing you need to stop immediately."

"Go on."

"Your feud with dirty energy companies needs to stop. You are to cease any further legal action against them. They serve a function in these last days of planet Earth. They are the catalyst that brings us to the brink of destruction. You need to let them."

"I couldn't. Not in good conscience. My shareholders-"

"Our future is not here in the dirt, Max. Our future is out there." The traveller motioned above, to the sky beyond the ceiling. "Our future is in the stars. The only way humanity will grow wings is if it is pushed out of the nest, and the only way to do that is to destroy the nest. We will not leave it willingly."

Maximillian exhaled. "You don't know what you're asking me to do."

"I know exactly what I'm asking you to do. I know how hard it is, but you also don't have a choice. Not if you care about the future of humanity. The stars call us. That's what you need to focus on. Look beyond the blue horizon and into the stars. Your name, your legacy, will live forever."

The traveller retrieved the device from the table and turned off the floating display. He stood, sucked down the last dregs of his coffee, then headed towards the front door.

"That's it?" Maximillian called after the traveller.

"That's it. This homeless vagrant thanks you for your hospitality."

Maximillian took a sip of his coffee, placed it roughly on the table and headed after the traveller. He stood in the doorway, one hand clutching the frame. He called after him.

"What's your name?" Maximillian shouted after him.

The traveller stopped on the paved walkway, hands in his pockets. He turned back towards Maximillian, then grinned. "The name's Jaxon. And I know you'll make the right choice. I wouldn't exist, otherwise."

Jaxon pressed a button on the side of his watch's face. There was a bright flash of light, then he was gone. A dark smear on the paved walkway was the only evidence he had ever been there.

Maximillian closed the front door and headed to his study. He had some calls to make.

# RENDEZVOUS AT ALEXGAIA
## Jeanette O'Hagan

"Operative 2679, for your safety, please remain confined."

Dana yanked the medi-support line from her arm and pressed her thumb against the well of blood. Her last mission came close to killing her, but she wasn't an invalid yet. She refused to stay cooped up like an injured space-chicken a moment longer. She slid her legs over the edge of the medipod and stood.

The room spun in a dizzy rush and her legs wobbled beneath her.

"Blast it to Haedis and back."

She pushed a splayed-out hand against the titanium-alloy wall for support and waited for her world to stop spinning. The artificial gravity on Prometheus Base was not quite Nardva-standard, but her sudden disorientation was more likely due to the left-over effects of whatever cocktail of narcs and heal-agents the auto-med program had pumped into her bloodstream.

Frag it, she hated the needles and the intrusion. The high-tech reminded her of the Consortium. Is this what Neon felt when they'd upgraded him? She slammed her fist into the wall, pain shooting into her wrist. No, she wouldn't think about that. He was gone, an empty shell. Like her sister and her parents. She would take down the Consortium piece by piece, even if it meant selling her organs or her soul, but she couldn't do it recuperating in the med-bay.

"Operative 2679, your treatment regime is not completed. Please return to your medipod at once or med-security will be informed."

Dana gritted her teeth at the faux-concern of the auto-med's disembodied voice. Regaining her balance, she dragged a set of standard issue garb from the overhead locker and pulled them on, the silver synthocloth conforming to her curves.

"Operative 2679..."

"My name is Dana, you perfidious lump of alloy and virtual circuits."

"... for your safety, please..."

She grabbed her plasma pistol and blasted the auditory outlet, savouring the crackle and fizz of disappearing sound. "re... tu... rn..."

Silence.

Somewhere outside, a high-pitched alarm sounded. Let it.

Dana prised open the automated door and stumbled into the long grey corridor. The alarm sounded louder here, an annoying, whining blare. She knew this base like the inside of her EVA suit. Pushing herself into a shambling run, her muscles finding the memory of the station's gravity, she headed to the Operations Room. She had a mission to complete, whether Controller Zaphron accepted that or not.

"You can't go in there, Operative."

"Then atomise me."

Dana pushed past the cadet and through the doors, stepping into a large circular chamber. The recessed lights were subdued and the view port shuttered against the curve of Woden's swirling gas clouds.

Three people stood clustered around the holo-pedestal, leaning in, eyes fixed on the rotating image; old Zaphron, a fidgety woman in the white synthocloth of a tech, and the back of a tall person that seemed familiar. Above them, a hologram of the sun system with its spread of ten planets glowed in an eerie maroon-purple. Only a pitiful few blinking green lights showed areas free of the Consortium blight.

Dana took a deep breath of recycled air. Defeating the giant conglomerate seemed impossible, but Neon had carried her along with his passion. Now he was gone. What was so important about the Infinity Cube that he'd sacrifice his personality, his memories, his freedom for it? The thought of her friend and teammate converted into a mechanised servant of the Consortium cut through her like a plasma-blade.

"Dana... what are you doing here?" Zaphron turned from surveying the holoimage, white eyebrows beetled over his bony nose.

Dana stood straight. "Operative 2679 reporting for duty, sir."

"Has the auto-med given you clearance?"

"Blast it, Zaphron, how many experienced operatives are left? I'm ready and willing to kick some Consortium butt."

The tall, familiar figure turned towards her. "It is precisely such reckless and negligent behaviour that scuttled your last two missions."

Dana stiffened, her teeth on edge at his recognisable and cultured voice, as smooth as Utonian synthacol. Tamper it down and double blast it, when had Zaphron brought Avonis on the mission? She had never wanted to see his blue, snooty nosed face again, not since the fiasco at Rama B.

She pushed the words through clenched teeth. "My last mission was not a failure."

A smirk appeared on that too-handsome face. "The

loss of Neon, our so-called best operative, the total destruction of your shuttle—I'd hate to see your definition of failure."

Heat scorched up her face. How could Avonis dismiss Neon's absorption with such cool derision? Her muscles trembled in an effort not to punch that superior smirk off his face. "We delivered the target."

Zaphron cleared his throat. "Ah yes, if we could focus, compadres. Despite regrettable losses, Dana has retrieved the Infinity Cube, and she has a point, Avonis, we need every last operative. We should focus on the next task."

"Which is?" Dana asked.

"Discovering what the Cube does and how best to use it for the cause."

"You don't know how to use it?" Both Dana and Avonis spoke at once, their words echoing off the walls of the chamber.

"Then how do you know it's important?" Avonis demanded.

"Can't your techs take it apart?" Dana added.

Zaphron gestured to the rotating holo-image of the titanium-grey cube Dana had lifted from the exclusion vault only Narv-days ago.

"Neon was convinced of its importance." Zaphron held up his hand as Avonis opened his mouth. "And what star-net communications we've been able to intercept confirm his confidence. Our intel has assessed a 99.978% probability that it is pivotal."

Then what was the problem? "So, dissect it."

"Typical." Avonis' refined face wrinkled into a sneer.

"Compadres, please." Zaphron spread out his hands. "Quite apart from the fact that our techs are convinced 'dissecting' it would set off a fail-safe self-destruct, it is made from a titanium-zirinium alloy."

"Eject it into the sun."

"Avonis, destroying it may ruin our last chance of taking down the Consortium. We have to open it."

"Bury it in a vault."

"We suspect it contains a tracking device. However deep we bury it, the Consortium will eventually find it. A cyborg armada is headed our way. Estimated time of arrival 64.6 Narv-hours."

Only the hum of the ventilation system and the shuffle of the tech's feet filled the room. There had to be something she—they—could do.

Avonis folded his arms, his face grim. "So, whichever way we look at it, we're neck deep in space junk."

The tech cleared her throat. "There is one clue to the Cube's function." She pointed to an etched symbol outlined with gold-titanium alloy on each of the six sides of the cube.

Dana squinted at the symbol. It looked like a kid's stick-figure drawing. "What does it mean?"

"We don't know."

Dana had seen figures like this before, a long time ago. "It ... could be a script."

"How would a refugee from a back eddies zone know that?" Avonis drawled.

The tech waved a hand. "The operative is right. Our best guess is that it's the script of a long dead language."

Avonis smiled grimly. "And the Consortium has systematically atomised or wiped all ancient artefacts and historical documents. Only their synthesised version of history is allowed."

"A people without history is easier to control, yes, but there is one place."

Dana felt a frisson of recognition. "Alexgaia Central Depository. I thought it was a myth, Zaphron,"

"No, it's not, just well hidden. Security is tight but

we have a contact, a tech-acolyte, inside. With two moons in alignment three Narv-days hence, we have an opportunity to slip through a weakness in the security net and transmit a couple of operatives in."

Dana met Avonis' almond-shaped eyes and nodded. It would be risky, suicidal even, but right now she didn't care. She had to ensure that Neon's absorption into the Consortium hadn't been pointless. She was in.

The all-body tingling dispersed as Dana materialised in a small, crammed room. Avonis solidified almost on top of her. She checked that she had all her digits and other appendages in the dim light and sighed with relief. She hated the disembodied feel of the transmit.

A short, tubby man in the long robes of a Depository tech-acolyte, switched off the homing signal and beckoned. "Quick, this way. I've disabled the surveillance in this section, but it won't be long before servobots come to check the lack of transmission." Sweat beaded the apple-green skin of the man's bald head. From the Karan Spice Islands, then.

"Come on." The acolyte ducked into a long dark corridor. They followed.

"I thought your order and our organisation would have common cause against the Consortium," Avonis whispered.

The acolyte looked over his shoulder. "Our order doesn't like rebels. Besides, there are rumours that the Abbess is negotiating with the Consortium, certain concessions for protection and special privileges."

Dana snorted. "Might as well negotiate with a black hole."

The info-monk shrugged his rounded shoulders.

"Takes aeons for a star-eater to consume a galaxy. In the meantime, there are perks for those in the know." His flabby face hardened. "The Consortium's attempt to corrupt the order needs to be stopped. The sacred repository is too important. Now shush." The sound of footsteps echoed through the ancient building. "In here, hurry."

The room had a musty odour mixed with a vanilla-like smell that stirred a long forgotten image of playing with her sister. Dana shook the ghosts from her head, focusing on the present.

They crouched behind a console until the tech-monks passed by.

"Show me the symbol." The acolyte's hands were shaking. He shoved them into the sleeves of his robe.

Avonis flicked the switch on his communicator and a holo-image projected in the space in front of him. "Does it mean anything, or are we on a wild asteroid chase?"

Dana held her breath, to not sneeze in the dusty air.

The monk tilted his head from side to side, his forehead wrinkled with concentration. He air-typed as strips of glowing blue letters whipped above the console. His eyes narrowed and he reversed the strip backwards. "Ah, yes, southern Eldane, an uncommon variant found in the Lonely Isles." A swipe of his index finger and the symbol enlarged.

"Seleste!" Dana's fingers tingled. She'd visited the Isles as a child, one of her parents' interminable placements. "What does it mean? A letter, an anagram?"

The monk dotted the air and a flexi-film flipped from the outlet. It had a series of numbers embossed on it. "I have no idea. It's a pictograph." A whining noise echoed from the corridor outside. "The servo-bots. I have to get back to my station. I can't be seen here."

"But can't you call up the meaning from the central computer?"

"That information is in the archives. Our order believes only the physical copies are sacred." He shoved the film and the home-beacon at Avonis. "Here, this is the number of the infodisc. You'll find what you need there."

He waved to the darkened room behind them and bolted out of the door.

The room was massive, with rows and rows of floor-to-ceiling shelves. They barricaded the door with furniture and crates of discs scattered around.

Dana flashed the bright light from her communicator along the shelves, looking at the numbers engraved on each stack.

Avonis glanced at the flexi-film. "We need Z-FAH 2017.VE. These symbols have some sort of order, if we could work it out."

"Alphabetical," Dana said. The dusty, pleasant smell grew stronger. Dana drifted toward the back, memories of running beneath the sunlit trees and swimming in the river battering against her defences; she, her older sister Terri, and Neon. Only he was Jerren then, before he joined the cause.

"Huh?"

"It's a way of ordering the letters." A nursery rhyme flittered to the top of her mind, "ABCD, EFG ..."

"I forget you came from an archaic economic zone."

"No, you didn't. You rub it in my face any chance you get. HIJ..." she hummed.

A banging and then a resounding crash came from the entrance. A wailing siren assaulted her eardrums. They were running out of time.

"It's got to be at the back." Dana pulled out her

plasma pistol and ran, her heart pounding in rhythm with her steps. A few tense moments and Avonis appeared behind her, following her lead. They ran along the stack, sounding letters. "Here, this shelf."

The smell of ozone and the sound of sizzling came from the barricaded doorway.

"They'll be here soon." Avonis caught his breath and waved his gun. "Numbers I know." His hand fluttered in front of the discs. "Here," he pulled out a black rectangle, oddly bulky.

They sprinted toward a holo-viewer against the wall.

A blur in on the edges of Dana's vision, she spun and atomised the spherical defence probe. Another swooped in from the right. She atomised it. Her pulse roared in her ears. "Press the beaming signal."

"The infodisc may not work with our equipment." He pushed the disc toward the slot. Another crash from the entrance, three more probes darted in between the stacks. She released a disrupter barrage, the sparkling lights spreading like a net. She shot down two probes and jumped to the side as a blast zapped her way from the third. "Come on, Avonis. We need to go."

"The fragged disc won't fit."

"Here, let me try." She whipped her plasma pistol around and took out another probe. "Cover me." She took the disc as Avonis shot down two more bots. "The guards will be here soon. It's a wonder they haven't used a bio-disrupter yet."

"It would wipe the sacred discs. The Consortium would, but not the Order."

The rectangle was too long and thick for the slot. It was soft, almost spongy. "Perhaps it has deteriorated." Like a sudden burst of sunlight, realisation struck. "It's a book."

"What?"

"A book, made of mashed trees and ink. Let's hope it's written in Common."

A group of heavily armed tech-monks rushed towards them from both ends of the stacks. A plasma blast singed her hair. She grabbed the home-beacon from Avonis' hand and pushed the button.

Dana collapsed back against the hull of the ship clutching the book. Avonis sprawled beside her.

She grinned at him and carefully opened the covers. "Ancient tech. Was still in use when I was a tot in our backwater." The pages were yellow and brittle and their scent transported her to a time when she was happy with her family and Jerren. She let out a soft breath. "The Eldane symbols are matched with an archaic form of Common. Difficult to decipher, yes, but not impossible. If the ancient symbol is the key to the Infinity Cube, we've found it."

"Maybe you're not such a complete liability."

Dana whipped her head up, about to retort.

There was a smile in Avonis' enigmatic eyes. "Even your rustic background came in handy."

Dana snorted. Fancy Avonis melting enough to give her a back-handed compliment. She pushed herself to her feet, cradling the book, and eyed the gleaming rehydrator. "Better request the coordinates to the new base while I find a safe place for this."

For the first time in days, she felt her spirits lift. Maybe Neon's sacrifice hadn't been for nothing. Perhaps, just perhaps, they held the key to take down the Consortium.

# THE GIFT
## Fiona Emily

The pedals creak beneath her feet.

*Don't stop. Keep going.*

Siquia glances up at the clock. It's ticking down way too slow. More energy drains with every passing second. She pushes harder, forcing the pedals to move. Lactic acid pools in her lower limbs. She wants to stop so badly, but she can't.

Stopping is no option.

Three o'clock looms, the finish line not far off, but still minutes away. If she doesn't meet quota she'll be out, and this job is everything; the only income for her family and their only protection against the cold. There are too many people on the waiting list ready to take her place, too many others facing the same desperation to survive.

She looks up, needing a distraction from the pain. Glass stretches out above her, an attempt to capture every ounce of sunlight. One precious golden beam forces its way through the canopy of clouds, there for a fleeting second before it's swallowed by the hulking blanket that covers everything.

The already-grey room sinks deeper into shadow. There's no wastage of light down here in the turbine room. Energy is precious. Lighting is reserved for the important places, for important people.

Siquia's gaze flicks back to the red numbers on the wall. Two minutes. That's 120 seconds, completely doable, a small snippet of time in her seventeen-year existence—if she can just ignore the burning in her legs. She starts counting, hardly able to gasp a breath as the pain reaches intolerable levels.

In the midst of the pain, her stomach growls. What she wouldn't give for another bowl of tasteless pellets. For reasons she can't understand, this hunger feels different to what she's felt before. Her insides are empty, devoid of anything fulfilling. Her body is breaking itself down until she has nothing left.

This job is only a short-term solution. There's no way she can sustain all this activity, not on the rations supplied. Although fit and strong, she was already small, and after only two weeks she's lost valuable centimetres around her waist, making her more susceptible to the cold... How long will it be until she wastes away to nothing?

What will happen to her mother, father and sister, with winter coming?

The thought brings panic, a deep anxiety that has her legs working harder and faster, determined to fight off the inevitable disaster growing with every turn of the crank.

A loud buzzer sounds.

Her legs stop at once. They slip off the pedals, hanging limply in the air. It's time. Three o'clock. Finally. She drops her head, needing a moment to catch her breath. No, a moment is too short. A week is more likely for fighting off the exhaustion infused in her bones.

There's movement all around as the others climb off their bikes, finished with their production of energy for another day.

They make it seem so easy.

Except it's not.

Tears fill her eyes. Normally she'd fight them off but today, feeling so drained, she lacks the strength.

Her legs feel like dead things, unwilling to move after being pushed so far. The idea of trying to walk out of here, even if it is to return to her bed for a rest, is too much.

But she needs to go. The next shift is coming in. Her seat will be filled by someone else. It's a requirement that she leave.

Bracing herself, she swings a leg over and slides down off the bike. As her feet touch the ground, she expects her legs to take her weight. They don't. She grips the bike seat, needing to lean against it to gain balance.

She glances around, fearful someone witnessed her fumble. The bikes nearby are all vacant. Except one.

The one beside hers.

Him. The tall strong capable male, who looks like he was designed for this job. He's pedalled beside her every day for the past fortnight. They've never exchanged a word, but she's caught him watching her before.

Was he watching her? Or is it a coincidence that he's here?

Her body goes rigid, waiting, wondering if any moment he will call her out and expose her weakness to the guardians.

She was warned about such dangers. Those among the workers who seek out the weak, aiming to oust the newbies so their relatives might be next on the list. It was drummed into her by her parents. *Don't trust anyone, just put your head down and work hard.*

Seconds pass. The room is quickly emptying, making her presence notable. He's not going anywhere fast either, which is an ominous sign.

She waits breathlessly.

What is he going to do?

He glances her way once more. Then he shifts—

not towards the guardians as she feared, but towards the door.

Relieved air fills her lungs.

Maybe she's being overly dramatic. Maybe he was just concerned for her wellbeing, with no intention of causing any harm.

Either way, she's survived another day. That alone is worth celebrating. There's almost a spring in her step when she starts to walk. The feeling is quickly lost as her legs remind her of the workout they just endured. With every step out of the turbine room and into the hall, they feel heavier. She wills them to keep moving, anything to blend into the crowd of bald heads where she won't be noticed.

Part way down, her legs decide to quit. They go all wobbly. Her vision clouds and she knows she needs to sit or stop if she has any chance of making it to her room without incident.

Of course, there are no seats anywhere in the hall.

Weakness isn't tolerated here.

She leans against the wall, fumbling with the belt at her waist, hoping it's not obvious she was forced to stop.

Just a loose belt. Nothing to see.

Feeling a strange lurch within her gut, she glances up. Sure enough, there he is again, watching her.

A cold shiver passes down her spine.

No one else is left in the hall, just the two of them. He takes a step towards her. Then another. He doesn't look at her or say anything, deliberately keeping his head down as he moves, until he's standing in front of her.

She looks up. Their eyes meet. At once she's immersed in a set of pale blue eyes. Her mother used to describe the sky to her as a child before the clouds came. She could never imagine a space that big, full of such colour, especially when everything was clothed in so much grey. But in that moment, she knows it must have been something to behold.

Just as his eyes are.

His brow furrows. "You need to come with me."

It's not the greeting she was expecting, she was hoping more for a hello.

"Why?" she asks, unable to hide the suspicion that emerges.

"I want to help you."

Could it be that this stranger with eyes like the sky is being kind? She wasn't warned off kindness, but it's not something she's witnessed outside her own family. It's a cut-throat world, survival of the strongest. But does that mean kindness is dead? He could have called her out earlier, only he didn't.

So should she trust him?

He hooks his arm beneath her elbow before she can decide.

Touch. When was the last time someone actually stood this close? Two whole weeks without a word to anyone, without any hint of closeness, has been a vacuum of solitude.

Warmth fills her insides. It's easier to walk with assistance. The world has stopped spinning for now, but she still doesn't feel right.

It's good that the door to her room is up ahead. She sighs, relief pouring through her. All that doomsday thinking was a waste of energy. She made it through another day, only a few metres separating her from the safety of her bed. All because of this guy holding her up and his gift of kindness.

She looks up at him, a smile almost hitting her lips.

He's wearing a grim look. His gaze is fixed, not on the door up ahead that leads to her room, but at the guardian standing in the doorway.

Each step forward is no longer about him helping her get back to her room. She knows at once he's no different from any of the others.

A bitter tang rises up her throat.

Kindness *is* dead.

She pulls her arm free, willing her legs to work. There's a corridor up ahead. Scooting sideways, she heads down a random offshoot, anything to avoid the guardian and this stranger's obvious intent.

He's by her side in a heartbeat. "What are you doing?" His arm grips hers. He attempts to steer her back towards the guardian.

She resists. They come to a hostile stand still in the middle of the hall. "The least you could do is tell me the truth."

He says nothing. Not. One. Word.

"Isn't this the part where you say, I'm planning to turn you in?"

He keeps his lips clamped shut.

"If I lose this job, my family won't make it through the winter."

She watches him for any hint that her words have registered. Nothing crosses his face. Does he not have any feeling left?

He lets out a heavy breath. At last his brow wrinkles. "My brother needs a job. He has a... baby."

Siquia drops her head. Tears fill her eyes. He has family too. Of course he would fight for them, how can she blame him for that? But it doesn't stop the defeat twisting her insides, or the fear immersing her at the thought of her family facing the cold of winter with no income.

Her voice trembles. "I won't last long here, I know you see it. But please – *please* – let me stay just a little bit longer?"

She knows without waiting for his answer what he will say.

This is hopeless. She may as well have fallen back at the bike, rather than wasted the energy trying to pretend she is capable of this. The inevitable end has reached her sooner than expected.

"Here." He hands her a bottle of water. "If you crush up the pellets and drink them throughout the day, it will help with your blood sugar levels."

He steps back from her, eyes down. Then he walks away, abandoning her in the middle of the hall.

Bewildered, she watches his form retreat.

She expects him to stop at the guardian, to reveal her weakness. But he doesn't. He just keeps walking. She stares at the bottle in her hand, her hand shaking as she takes a sip. What comes out is definitely not just water. It's bitter and foul and hard to force down, but she does. The effect hits her instantaneously, like a blast of light.

# BAD HAIR DAY
## Julian St Aubyn Green

No one knows how it started or where it came from. No one was ready for it. All our technology and glorious war machines and they were no damned good. I used to enjoy watching zombie apocalypse movies until I was in one. Difference between reality and fantasy I suppose, is being cocooned in comfort and a voyeur to disaster. It sucks having to live in a world without all the things you once took for granted, like flicking a switch to turn on the light, or running water and food on demand.

Except it isn't zombies.

I've heard all the theories. Alien monster, bioweapon, something we disturbed, Mother Nature's revenge for us screwing her up. Personally, I don't think it's from this world. It's too weird. But Dad says that a parasite that bonds so successfully with its host probably evolved within the same biosphere. Yeah, he talks that way. He's a scientist. Industrial Chemist. Or he was before the world turned to shit.

We're trying to learn how to fight it. Because it's far worse than zombies. Zombies are stupid. That's how the hero wins in the end. Finds a way to trick them. Finds a way to hide somewhere until all the corpses fall over and civilisation starts again.

It's smart, but it doesn't talk. Not with its mouth anyway. We've read the notes left by people it's taken over. Hosts, victims, whatever. They plead, say they tried to kill themselves and it stopped them. We know, at a certain point, it starts communicating with its host. That's where we got its name: Follicle.

Only smart things have names.

Dad thinks it could communicate if it wanted to. The infected, when taken over, laugh insanely in that high pitch—like a hyena, black froth streaming from their eyes like tears. Long black glistening hair falling to their feet that moves on its own.

I heard it laugh for the first time on a television broadcast when we still had TV. Sent a shiver down my spine then and still does every time I hear it. Spread out across the city, echoing at us from every direction in the darkness. Used a telescope one night. Saw them all, up on rooftops, laughing and dancing. No, really. They were dancing, I swear it. Under the full moon like a witch's coven or something.

You don't see them during the day. They mostly come out at night. Mostly. Hell, that sounds familiar. Where was that from? Some movie. Whatever. Follicle just laughs as if the world is a joke.

It also likes certain kinds of animals. Mammals, animals with hair. I used to be a cat person. Guess that's over. I've never seen it in a bird or lizard. I found a rat in the garden today and killed it with a shovel. Was going to eat it until I saw the black strands, the wriggling hair. I put it in a plastic bag and threw it off the roof.

I found a big black hair on the back of my hand that afternoon. Ripped it out and swore when I poured bleach on my hand.

I can't move around as well as I used to. So Dad and Glen would climb down during the day and look for supplies in the city, while I tended the garden that keeps us alive.

Glen. God, I haven't wanted to write his name

because I can't think of him without the waterworks starting. Love of my life, father of the child inside me. Words aren't enough, even with the tears dripping off my nose.

Now it's just Dad, me, the baby inside me and this fucking uninvited parasite.

Dad has a theory that chemotherapy drugs might work. People lose their hair when they have chemotherapy. He's been stockpiling different chemo drugs, just in case. The drugs attack fast-growing cells within the body, and Follicle grows fast. Most people are gone in a week. Dad says he read somewhere that some of the drugs are okay to use beyond the first trimester. Didn't know which ones. Can't look it up. Google is gone.

Even after finding the hair, even after my temperature soared, I still didn't want to try them. I've seen my daughter on a scan, heard her heartbeat, felt her move. What a choice. Try and save my own life and maybe kill my unborn daughter in the process. Have to try. If there is a slim chance that the drugs will kill Follicle and leave my daughter alive, I have to take it.

I'm pretty out of it right now. Dad gave me something, trying to bring my temperature down. But I'm also numb. Emotionally numb, like it's happening to someone else. Dad's doing what he can, but I can see the despair in his face he's trying to hide. He's already lost Mum. Five years ago, the big C. If we go, he'll be alone. I don't know what he'd do, I'm afraid to ask. I have to stop now. Crying too much. Need to blow my nose.

I don't think the chemotherapy is working. Dad is hopeful. I haven't blacked out yet. Haven't heard anything in my head. No black froth coming out my eyes and no sign of black hair on my shaved head. But

I can feel slow changes. Dad wants to increase the dosage. Walk the tightrope between enough chemo to kill Follicle and not kill the baby.

He left the drugs by the bed. I told him I'd sleep on it. They are sitting there, mocking my fears right now. Fuck you chemo. Fuck you. You will hurt my baby if I take too much of you.

The change isn't painful, feels like a cold. Sore throat, temperature, itchy and bloodshot eyes. Maybe it is just a cold, or maybe it's the chemo drugs. God, I hope so, but I know I'm deluding myself.

It's in me. I'm infected.

If it was just me I think I'd kill myself. Just take the gun and end it. Dad can see it in my face. He said he doesn't want me to quit. Says we fight for our kids until we can't fight anymore.

He's been collecting the notes the victims leave behind, looking for clues. I'm not supposed to see them, he doesn't want me to read all the terrible things written on them, but I snuck downstairs and stole a few when he went out looking for supplies.

He was right. I should not have read the notes. They all start out like this one. Lucid, normal, or this new-world fucked-up version of normal anyway. Then every so often there's a word or two written in a different handwriting that doesn't match the context. Crazy shit. And you know just reading it that the writer didn't know it was there. That they'd skipped over it. I went back over what I've written. No crazy shit yet, so maybe the drugs are keeping Follicle contained.

Last one I read was by a man. Holed up somewhere in the city with his family when Follicle got into him. They didn't have a gun. Tried to kill himself with a knife and the hair gripped his arms. When that didn't work he asked his wife to do it for him. She couldn't do it either. Couldn't get close, every time she did, his hair would move and he didn't want her infected. The guy ended up locking himself in the basement and blacking out. Woke up in the kitchen lying in a pool of blood with his wife's decapitated head resting on his chest. Freaked out. Found his daughter in the fridge.

Then he said he heard the voice. Said it sounded like the little blue alien from that movie with the Hawaiian girl. Follicle swirling, can you hear the music? The many strands? Dancing so nice, red wetness so nice, chasing the food so fun.

Crazy shit, right?

I haven't heard the voice yet, but one thing I noticed. The voice doesn't appear until after you black out, and I haven't done that yet.

Time to walk the tightrope. Fuck you chemo.

God. I've never asked you for anything. I'm asking now. Please keep my baby safe.

I heard the voice for the first time today. Four weeks we kept it at bay with the chemo drugs. I knew it couldn't be long. Dad keeps flinching when he looks at me. My eyes have gone completely black and the two inches of stubble on my head is moving. But my daughter is kicking. She's alive.

WHY FOLLICLE STRAND SO SLEEPY? That's what I heard inside my head.

Asked Dad to handcuff me, told him to get the gun and keep it on him at all times. To wear his hazmat suit. I think I'm contagious now. I thought about the date. My daughter is due at Christmas. Halloween passed a few days ago. She might live if Dad cuts her out now. Babies have been born more premature than that and survived. But that was with modern medical care. How is Dad meant to manage? All by himself, no electricity. My baby will probably die if we try it. I want her to live. It's all I can think about now. She needs to live and go on living. She needs to survive this end of the world shit. You do anything for your kids. So, I'm going to do something crazy. I'm going to try and talk to it, like in the other notes. See if it'll write things down. I want to know if Follicle can be bargained with. I'm overdue for my chemo now, and I can feel the stubborn hair moving on my scalp again. It's time to try.

Follicle. Hey!

SLEEPY NO DANCE NOW.

Hey! I want to talk to you.

SHHH FOLLICLE NO HEAR SONG OF MANY STRANDS.

I'm trying to kill you Follicle.

WHAT IS KILL?

Dead. Cease to be. End.

YOU SILLY. FOLLICLE NOT END. TOO MANY STRANDS. FOLLICLE EVERYWHERE.

What does that mean? You. You inside me. I can kill you.

YOU NOT WANT FOLLICLE INSIDE? YOU NOT WANT DANCE AND SONG AND RED WETNESS TASTY?

No. I don't.

FOLLICLE NOT GO. FOLLICLE LIKE. FIND FOOD LATER. SLEEP NOW. CHANGE TIRING.

No. Talk to me dammit. You want to know why changing me is so hard? I have drugs to kill you, burn you out of me.

MANY TRY BURNY. MANY TRY STABBY AND BANG AND SPLODE. FOLLICLE SPREAD. FOLLICLE STRANDS STILL GROW. ALL OVER ROUNDNESS.

Wait. Are you connected to everyone you infect?

MANY STRANDS. ALL OVER BLUE GREEN ROUNDNESS. WHAT IS INFECT?

Infection. That's what you are. A parasite. You invade my body, and I kill you with the drugs. See the drugs Follicle? That's what you do, isn't it? See with the eyes when they go black. You've been trying to take me over. You normally only take a few days to take someone over. That's why you are taking longer with me, because of the drugs, and if I take enough, I kill you.

WHY NOT? END STRAND. FOLLICLE NOT CARE. FOLLICLE HAVE MANY STRANDS.

Because if I do I might kill my daughter. I'd cut her out if I could. But it's too soon. She won't survive.

WHAT IS DAUGHTER?

My child. Growing inside me. She's been growing inside me for seven months. Look. She's moving. She is alive. I want her to stay that way.

YOU HAVE TWO BEATS. ONE FAST ONE SLOW. FOLLICLE SEE THIS BEFORE. NOT KNOW WHAT MEAN. FAST BEAT IS TASTY.

Screw you. Touch her and die.

DAUGHTER NOT FOOD?

No. Not if you want to live.

WHAT MEAN?

I mean if you stop trying to take me over for a while, I'll let you live. I'll let you have me, I won't resist. I'll trade her life for mine.

WHY?

Because you do anything for your kids.

YOU WANT FOLLICLE SLEEP? FAST BEAT DAUGHTER LEAVE. THEN YOU TAKE BURNY DRUGS. KILL STRAND.

No. I think it might kill me to try. I can't undo what you've already done. I promise.

Hey! Answer me.

YES. FOLLICLE SLEEP TILL NEXT ROUND BRIGHTNESS. TILL FAST BEAT DAUGHTER GONE. THEN WE DANCE.

It kept its promise. It stopped trying to take me over

and I stopped taking the chemo drugs to give my daughter the best chance to be born healthy. Dad's been researching C-sections. Says he can do it. The only change in those four weeks was my hair grew fast; down to my waist. This morning, Dad noticed my eyes changed colour. Instead of solid black, there were these strange patches of moving white. We don't know what it means. We've never seen that before.

I tried talking to Follicle again and it didn't answer. Yelled inside my head to ask what was happening. Nothing. Tried pulling out a hair to wake it up, and when it came away in my hand, it was white. Platinum stripper blonde.

Dad agreed to do the C-section.

Numbed the skin, made the cut, and out she came, quiet as a mouse. No screaming. With a full head of long white hair that moved on its own. She turned and focused eyes of swirling black and white on me and smiled. And that's when the door crashed in and an infected burst into the room, laughing that hyena laugh.

I thought we were dead, but the hair on my head moved. And the hair on my daughter's head moved. Where it touched the infected he went from black to white like turning on the lights. And the man beneath the hair broke down and cried tears of joy. I heard him in my head. Just like I heard my daughter.

We're all connected.

Follicle sent more strands. There are dozens of Whitehairs now.

My daughter. Saviour of the fucking planet.

*Let's dance, Follicle.*

# THE FINAL AMBUSH
## Maria Caesar

It had been ten years since the alien species had first arrived on their planet, Tinaye. Ten long years of constant battles as the Tinayen inhabitants defended their homes from the intruders. Unfortunately, the Tinayens were losing the war. The alien forces were too powerful and their technology too great after plundering the resources from numerous other planets throughout the galaxy. In their wake, entire civilisations had been decimated.

As Tinaye's population slowly dwindled, the planetary leaders reluctantly made the decision to evacuate their beloved home-world. Departure zones were designated, well away from major cities, in an attempt to give the fleeing transport ships a chance to escape. As soon as the aliens discovered the location of one departure zone, a new destination was elected and updated co-ordinates were provided to the terrified populous by means of crude radio communication.

Making the journey towards the departure zones was treacherous, particularly when evacuees gathered together prior to boarding. In order to protect the civilian population, combat teams were assigned, both on the ground and with air cover.

Jonathan Mayamiko was the leader of the on-ground defence teams. He had swiftly risen through the ranks after successfully escorting several large groups of evacuees. However, the final group was the largest.

Hundreds of thousands of people were lined up, tugging the hands of children and carting luggage as the pace of the queues moved painfully slowly. John stood upon a rocky outcrop whilst monitoring the crowd, concerned that they were going to be there all day.

"Halt! No more are allowed to board this ship!" One of the soldiers on the ground announced. Others stepped forward to prevent a large group from continuing onto the gangways.

There were no complaints. More ships were on their way, ready to dock side by side, linking onto the temporary loading platforms that lined the ridge.

Although things appeared to be moving along smoothly, John felt agitated. If they had been able to utilise a larger and flatter area, then they could have evacuated quicker. Instead, the fleeing inhabitants were limited to this narrow area, situated between two large rocky hills and ending at the edge of a very steep cliff.

The metallic doors on the side of the transport ship slid shut before the craft disconnected from the dock and headed off to space. Although capable of landing on the ground, the site they had chosen prevented this option. To counteract this problem, the flight crews made their crafts hover for boarding. It was a risky manoeuvre but so far the temporary loading platforms remained firm.

"Red Team members check in," John instructed through his communicator.

They had done a radio-check barely fifteen minutes earlier but John was on edge. Something wasn't right. He couldn't shake off the feeling that they had been forced to use this zone for a reason – like animals being herded into cages.

He took some consolation that his team had been able to position the laser canons beforehand. Also, with this location being the final collection point, John had an additional trick up his sleeve.

"Red Two standing by," came back the first report.

"Red Three standing by," another reported – followed in quick succession by the next four guards.

"Red Eight: check in now," John instructed when Red Eight failed to report. "Red Eight check in now," John repeated before indicating to Red Six and Seven that they should investigate.

The entire team went on alert. John watched as Red Six and Seven moved over towards Red Eight's last known position. The sound of loud blaster shots were heard as a team of enemy foot soldiers appeared on the ridge. Behind them rose a massive enemy craft, fully armed and ready for attack, with several smaller ships flying alongside.

The enormous alien ship crept over the horizon. It was ten times larger than any of the other alien space-crafts John had previously encountered but it also moved twice as slow. It was the one advantage the Tinayens had over their enemies – that their crafts didn't adapt well to the heavy atmosphere and strong gravity fields of Tinaye – but what the aliens lacked in speed, they made up for with firepower.

"Get those people on board the transport ships now!" John ordered as the next trio of ships prepared to dock.

The Tinayen vessels were barely in place as the doors slid open and platforms were extended to link to the docks, granting entry to the tide of evacuees. The people, seeing the enemy so close, panicked and ran. It was chaotic down there. Family members were separated. Weaker ones were knocked down and trampled.

"Fire the canons!" John ordered. His command was

immediately followed by a score of thunderous blasts that punctured the side of the enemy ship. They destroyed it but their elation was short lived. Two more ships followed behind and they aimed their weapons at the helpless transports.

"Where is Blue Team?" John shouted into the microphone – Blue Team was the code name for the combined squadrons of fighter pilots assigned to the evacuation.

"They're in battle behind that next ridge," came the dreaded reply.

It was an ambush, just as John had feared. His one and only aim was to rescue as many citizens as possible.

The canons destroyed a second enemy ship as it swooped to protect the mother ship. The smaller vessel buckled and exploded nearby, sending a momentary heatwave in John's direction. Seconds later, opposition fire from the mother ship struck the central transport vessel. The wounded craft dipped and swayed, losing control before colliding with the one positioned on its right. Both transport ships prematurely broke away from the docks; any unlucky souls that were still on the boarding platforms plummeted to their death. A second series of enemy fire caused both crafts to explode.

There was still one last Tinayen vessel intact and able to be boarded.

"Protect that transport ship!" John ordered as he raced forwards into battle.

His body armour made him look twice as tall and gave him a hundred times his strength and speed. The boosters beneath his boots propelled him upward. He launched himself at an enemy soldier, willing to fight to the death.

The battle was fierce. The enemy were relentless in their attack. At last the final group of civilians boarded the transport ship. The vessel closed the hatch. It moved away, dodging enemy fire as it successfully disappeared into the sky.

Back on the battlefield, there were only two members of Red Team still alive: John and Red Three. With no more civilians left on the planet's surface, there was only one more task to achieve: Destroy the enemy!

It was time to bring John's final trick into play. Hidden in the surrounding hills were a series of explosives. Every member on Red Team was able to detonate them as there was no guarantee that John would survive this far. Red Three nodded at John. The detonators had been built into the metallic bands on their wrists. The pair raised their hands in unison as if to look at their wristwatches to read the time.

At that moment, an enemy craft appeared, aiming its weapons at them. They were so close he could see the flight crew on the bridge. The mother ship was hovering not far behind, exactly where John needed it to be. Perhaps evacuating at this ridge had been a good decision after all.

John smirked triumphantly. "Mission accomplished," he muttered as he activated the detonator. The last thing he saw was the mother ship sustaining major damage before crashing to the ground.

# DRAGONS IN AREA 51
## Kasper Beaumont

Mega Containment Room, 2193 A.D. The laser shield crackled into place around the white crystalline walls of the lab, strengthening the double containment, positive-pressure isolation room. Two very different but equally anxious people entered the outer chamber wearing hazmat suits. They waited for the green light to show above the airlock before performing their retinal scan.

As the door slid shut behind them, Major Petra Dirk and Dr Farin Rasheed exchanged glances and nodded.

"Have we truly created dragons with genetic manipulation and splicing?" Petra's voice sounded deep through the microphone clipped into her audio-processing implant. Usually calm and emotionless, bile rose in her throat in expectation of what awaited them. Her hands shook inside the heavy prion-retardant gloves. Her heart's pulsation thundered in her ears. The hazmat mask fogged for a moment before the breathing apparatus cleared her visor. Petra drew a deep breath and assumed her role as the dominant in this professional relationship.

Beads of sweat dripped down Doctor Rasheed's face behind his visor. He nodded several times and bowed. "It is a relief to finally be finished after years of being sworn to secrecy." Petra noticed the flush of anticipation on his mocha-coloured skin. His voice sounded strained even with his New Indo-Emirates accent. "The President will reward us for our success."

Petra glanced at the incubator. *Reward for success and execution for failure.* She shuddered.

A scratching sound was heard.

Their eyes darted to the green eggs, resting in a heated bed of swirling white plasma. An egg as long as Petra's forearm jumped and bumped the next egg, which toppled onto the third in a domino effect.

"Major, hatchment is close." The doctor's eyes shone with excitement as he righted the fallen eggs and pushed them back into place. He picked up a pair of tweezers from the sterile blue drape on the table and tapped on the exterior of the middle egg.

The scratching became more frequent and intense, culminating in a shell breach.

Petra activated her helmet recorder through voice recognition. "Viz on."

Nearby, the crowd of dignitaries displayed their impatience by fidgeting, whispering and tapping their pens as they waited in the auditorium. A cheer erupted as the 3D holo-image appeared before them in full colour. The room grew silent as one green egg exploded, revealing a dark green reptile standing in the nest and stretching its wings.

Wiping birth fluid and egg-shell from his mask, Dr Rasheed gasped at the uncharacteristic maturity of the newborn. It raised a wide muzzle into the air and let out three high pitched cries.

The major and doctor slapped their hands to the sides of their masks, but were unable to mute the deafening screeches. The tweezers fell to the floor a second before both people collapsed to their knees.

Petra screamed.

The second egg exploded and another dragon emerged and joined in the intense screeching.

Flying shards of eggshell shattered Petra's mask. Wincing, she pulled it free from her head before she clapped her hands to her ears.

The mask's viz-recorder continued collecting footage, now sideways on the floor.

The third egg exploded and a thick shard of shell penetrated Dr Rasheed's suit at his neck. His head hit the floor as blood spurted from a severed artery, splattering the crystalline ceiling. His eyes bulged with terror and blood leaked from the corner of his mouth. The dragons pounced upon the decapitated scientist, tearing apart his suit and ripping his skin with sharp claws. They breathed sparks of fire on the flesh before devouring it.

Petra gagged on the horrific sight and the stench of burning flesh. She doubled over and lost her lunch on the floor.

"Help! Send in the extermination team." The major's voice was weak and gasping but her order reached the waiting soldiers in the next chamber.

Sirens blared and the ceiling glowed red with emergency lighting.

The heavy thud of boots made the floor vibrate as twelve experienced battle troopers entered the room carrying flame throwers. They lined the walls, maintaining strict eye contact with their major, awaiting the order.

Petra hauled herself to her feet and glanced at the corpse. The dragons met her eye, then something changed. It was not a colour-shift so much as a camouflage. One second they were there, dark green with raised wings, the next second they were invisible.

"Gone." Petra's word hung in the air and a few soldiers in the troop swore. She blinked rapidly several times. Then they heard flapping wings.

"Torch the room. Do not let them escape."

The soldiers shuffled to one side at a hand signal from their captain, then the entire chamber was doused in flames. The guns moved back and forth from ceiling to floor as they retreated through the doorway.

The air thinned as oxygen was consumed in the inferno. Everything in the room was destroyed; audio-viz equipment, test tubes, furniture, even rats in a cage awaiting their fate as the dragons' intended first meal.

Coughing at the smoke, Petra crouched and exited through the ante-room, followed by the soldiers. The flame-throwers ceased as they left.

They returned to the auditorium where a dazed Major Petra Dirk would be expected to deliver the news of their failure. She hung her head and shuffled her feet, at a loss for an explanation.

The dragons waited a long time before they emerged from the ruined shell of the laboratory. The heat from the flames had caused them to grow and they were now as tall as a human, with a wingspan even wider. Their scales had hardened in the inferno.

And so had their hearts.

# DELIRIUM
## L. G. Dalton

Sorrel shivered in the dry, chilly cave. She studied her sleeping men in the dim torchlight, listening to their breathing, ready to cover their mouths should they whimper with dreams. Their slumber was restful, considering their accommodations. Ducking terrorist gunshots in the dark was not on her entertainment list. Her team slumbered on, secure in her ability to keep them safe. Neil showed signs of stirring. He would take point and she could nap. She turned to Steve sleeping beside her and checked his shoulder. By the light of a hand-held torch, she had removed the bullet and stitched the wound closed. The coldness and dryness of the cave should keep it free of infection, but she needed to check it when there was better light. His breathing was steady and his hand warm. Her fingers rested against his pulse.

She sighed. Her breath barely disturbed the air in front of her mouth but reverberated in her ears. Damn all cold mountains. Her shivers grew stronger, and her teeth clenched to stave the chattering. As the team doctor, she was the one person who could not sicken. Though she trusted her men's first aid skills with injuries, they were not the best nurses with the sick. Calais, the other female on the team, was worse than the men. Give her a piece of wood, and the girl made a workable firearm in half an hour. Give her a sick child to care for and you had two sick people on your hands. She wriggled on her thin cushion of air.

Curse the Army's inferior equipment. The inflatable bed she sat on offered little protection from the hard cave floor. It merely slowed the leaching of body heat. The thick parka and Kevlar jacket provided a measure of warmth and comfort against the cave wall.

She flicked open her wristwatch's leather cover and glanced at it. Time crawled on microscopic lead feet. She took a deep breath. Every inhalation slid down her throat with the delicate softness of sandpaper embedded with glass shards. Her lungs burnt and her ribs were mini boa constrictors adding to the torture.

Sorrel cocked her head, listening to the night. In the thin mountain air, sound carried a good distance. The ghostly night wind howled across the cave's mouth. Shivers and chills slid along her spine with the precision of a xylophone maestro. Her shivering recommenced with renewed vigour.

A fire would be nice but unwise. They had no wood to burn, and it risked fouling the air. She had no desire to die of asphyxiation. The cave was deep enough to hide them from passing eyes and high enough for them to stand upright without braining themselves. Her head fell backwards against the wall. Thank the heavens for helmets.

Sorrel stared across the cave and into darkness. She knew better than to close her eyes. Tired as she was, she dared not sleep. She resorted to a childhood game of staring into nothing and waiting to see what images formed. Her favourites from that long ago time rarely appeared. She stared at the wall opposite her. Clad in shades of black, as shadow lay upon shadow, the wall contorted and swayed, pulsating in time with her jagged breathing.

The shivering increased. Her teeth were in danger

of cracking, so tight were they clenched. Black, red, and white spots formed and danced a tuneless gay gavotte halfway between her nose and the opposite wall. Dark curtains swayed at the edges and covered the cave's mouth. More coloured spots joined the dance and grew into sparkles. The gavotte turned into an energetic jig, and then into a riotous rollicking reel.

Sparkles coalesced into their separate colours. Shimmery masses grew, widened and lengthened until they were roughly humanoid in shape. They grew and shrank according to their own whims and in time to music only they heard. Squat gave way to elegant and tall. Wings appeared and vanished between one shiver and the next. Arms undulated, linked then unlinked. The cave filled with fantastical beings intermingling in an intricate pattern. They separated and frolicked around the cave and each of the sleeping men. The black shimmer cavorted in front of her, filling her vision.

"That never happened," she breathed. A wisp of raw air slipped into her mouth. She covered her mouth with her gloved hand and muffled a harsh cough, then reached for her water canteen and sipped the cold water. The water numbed as it trickled down her throat. Icicles slid along her gullet to settle in her stomach.

The shimmer glimmered at her. *"Look deeper."*

Sorrel bit hard on her Kevlar covered knuckle. The baritone voice regularly soothed her into sleep as a child. This time it flowed over and around her.

*"Tell me what you see."*

The liquid voice slid into her ears like warm oil. It whisked her back to the days when everything was good and wonderful, and Dad slew dragons with a fierce scowl. Her lips kicked upwards at the corners.

*"Sorrel."*

The voice insisted she pay attention. Her focus sharpened on the black scintillant. She watched fascinated, as the chest area illuminated and scenes scrolled across the surface.

Her team appeared garbed in form-fitting uniforms among similarly dressed men and women. The uniforms were bright, patterned and definitely not Army issue. Weapons resembling rifles, but looked at home in any science fiction movie, were in their hands. Her team held their weapons in a non-threatening position, still poised for action. They were moving through thick jungle, pushing purple tree fronds aside. A largish, three-toed creature lumbered out of the yellow brush, its ochre fur standing on end as it hissed. Yellow, stalked eyes glared menace at the intrusion.

Sorrel blinked and rubbed her eyes and the illusion vanished. The wall bowed and flexed with each razored breath. Its darkness varied in intensity. She swore carvings climbed from floor to ceiling. Blinking cleared her blurring vision. Her mouth dropped open at the image hovering before her.

A laughing Calais stood in the midst of four men, each of them smiling at her in wonder and intimate adoration. There was peace and happiness about her, something she had not known for over half her lifetime. Calais, the wolf-who-walked-alone, had found kindred spirits. But four men? If anyone could benefit from a ménage relationship, it would be Calais. Sorrel smiled faintly, pleased for her friend, and then blinked. Calais was speeding above land on a vehicle resembling a cross between a motorbike and hovercraft. The girl cradled a person in front of her. Sorrel was as grim as the two men lifting the injured from the hovering machine. A third stony male waited until the vehicle settled on the ground and Calais dismounted. Then he shook her by the shoulders until her teeth rattled. Someone was angry and upset. Calais retaliated with a well-placed fist to the stomach before mounting the steps of a log ranch house. Sorrel winced in sympathy. What did he expect? Calais did whatever she felt she had to.

The scene faded, replaced by another. This time the focus was the men.

Slender-built Neil laughed and arm-wrestled a brawny Viking. They sat in a tavern with a huge crowd yelling encouragement to both men. Tony and Jon watched his antics, their arms curled around their wives' waists. The women sat on tall barstools chatting to other women straight out of Dark Age Europe, Ancient Greece, Feudal Japan and Dynastic Egypt. All the women ignored Neil's antics and the men's goading. A cheer went up as Neil forced the golden Viking's arm onto the table. One of the watching females clapped, delighted. The others merely shrugged and kept talking. Neil rose, and joined Jon and Tony, spoke briefly to them and then left. Sorrel followed him as he left the tavern and walked grey-painted hallways, his heels lightly tapping on the metal flooring.

Where was Steve? Panic reared up, and she started hyperventilating. She still held his hand, his pulse steady and strong against her fingers. Sorrel breathed slowly, calming her erratic heartbeat. This was just a dream. Loner Calais, the heart of four men? Slender, lightweight Neil arm wrestling a Viking? Tony and John drinking with their wives? It had to be a dream.

Soft laughter cuddled her. *"Keep watching."*

The scene shifted to show Steve teaching a group of people of all ages the fine art of cricket. Sorrel relaxed. Steve enjoyed teaching cricket to the less informed. Wherever he was, he had a rapt audience. Lesson finished, he walked with the group to where his wife waited with refreshments. They were in a park with purplish matting underfoot. Flowering plants the size of trees reached skywards, bordering the park. Steve stopped and glanced skywards.

Sorrel followed his gaze and stared at stars. Where on earth...? No matter how hard she tried, she did not see one familiar constellation. They stood in a huge domed structure watching stars whizz by. Planets, moons, comets and asteroids loomed large then shrank into nothingness. In the distance, a nebula lighted the surrounding sky. It grew ever larger and brighter as it came nearer. She juddered as if crossing a speed bump. Then she was inside the towering cloud of gas. The soft rain of storming dust on metal assailed her. The stars sped past faster than a sideshow alley ride. The roller coaster ride slowed as three suns came into view. Sorrel shook her head. She was no astronomer beyond a cursory interest in the stars of her homeland. The star systems were in motion with moons orbiting planets, planets orbiting each other, and the suns orbiting a central area.

The scintillant chest rippled as another image appeared. A gargantuan metallic ball glided along stellar streams flowing throughout the combined system. It was a beautiful sight. The giant gimbals surrounding the central orb moved idly, as if it slowed to gain its bearings.

Sorrel blinked. The scene shifted and slew to reveal a new image starring her. She stood shoulder to shoulder with a male garbed in full regalia, gold braid strewn from shoulder to shoulder and across the length of his chest. Much less gold elegantly decorated her simpler regalia. They were co-leaders from the arrangement of the people standing behind them and their outfits. Steve, Jon, Neil and Tony were near her, mingling with others. She studied herself through another's eyes, from a frontal and elevated vantage. The picture was disconcerting, with her body encased in a green-blue-lavender bright aura.

From regalia to scrubs and she worked furiously to stop someone from bleeding out. Her tunic was liberally splattered with the brown of dried blood. The scene did not reveal if she was successful. Instead, it showed her slumped at a desk when strong arms lifted and carried her away. Tender hands stripped the stained tunic away and tucked her naked into a bed. She watched fascinated, as her hands crept around a strong neck and she raised her head for a kiss. Wow! That was new. She was yet to find the man she wanted to share her life with. Her finger caressed his brow, tracing features. What was with the forehead ridges? They extended from the outer orbital ridge and winged upwards to the hairline. The tattoos wound their way down his strong neck and flowed along an arm and his chest in curlicues unlike any tribal tatt she knew. He curled her against his chest, holding her, urging her to sleep. His fingertips fluttered across her eyes.

"What?" she murmured perplexed. She grimaced and ceased her game. It was bordering on the nonsensical. Her eyes closed and then flew wide open. She must not fall asleep!

*"Your new life. Your work here is done. Sleep now. When you awake you will have the knowledge you need to start your new work. Time will have passed, but everything you and your team need will be waiting for you, including family. Sleep. The universe is unfolding and everything is as it should be."*

If she heard *Desiderata* being mangled, she was definitely suffering a malady. Her head fell backwards against the cave wall.

"Shortness of breath, cold shivers, hallucinations, talking to self, now paracusia. Must be altitude sickness." A soft cough escaped. She grimaced. Lord, her chest ached, and each breath shredded her throat.

A murmured chortle cocooned her. She floated from the ground. Strong hands upon her shoulders guided and manoeuvred her around. The wall opposite her was no more. She glided along a cave hallway. Dim wall carvings of foreign gods flickered into life and faded in flaring lights. Firm hands stilled her struggles as she twisted to reach and alert her team.

*"All is as it should be, Sorrel. Sleep and rest."*

A spectral hand covered her eyes. Darkness enveloped her in warm, silky, woollen blankets. Yep, she was dying and on her way to Purgatory. Her mind blanked, the shivers ceased... and her eyes closed.

# THE TIME-TRAVELLER'S DATE
## Jodie Lane

Michelle straightened from her crouch as the blue haze dissipated and the Jump Room of 2617 AD appeared around her. She cross-checked her arrival with the time display on the wall, mentally logged it in her chronokinetor, and popped the time-travel device from her hand.

"How'd I go?" she called up to the control room. The technician fist-bumped the glass with a grin. Michelle returned the smile, exhausted but elated. Getting a young Charles Darwin onto the Beagle had been the easy part. Checking in on him later in life had required subtlety but, as his publications made their way out into nineteenth century Earth, she was confident of her success in repairing the timeline.

"Commissioner is on the com for you from Vivaldis." Another technician escorted Michelle from the Jump Room to Medic Bay. "Says you can report in while you get your post-mission checks."

As blood tests were taken and scans were done, a hologram flickered into view above the computer nearby.

"Congratulations, Agent Michelle. Another successful mission. That makes, what, ten now?" The hologram was an older, brown-skinned woman with a hard, military expression.

"Citizen Hera! You're Commissioner now?

Congratulations!"

Hera smiled, a forced look on a naturally grim face. "I was promoted while you were away. Thank you. I look forward to taking the Agency into a new era of influence. Before you give me your report, I want to advise that you have been issued two months of leave, on Earth or back on Vivaldis—as you prefer. You've done exceptionally well for our youngest Agent, but we don't want you to burn out."

"That's very kind of the Agency but I'm feeling great, really. Once this mission's fatigue wears off, I'll be right to prep for the next."

The hologram blurred as Hera shook her head. "There is a lot of work coming up soon but other Agents can handle it. Truth to tell, Agent Michelle, there's a bit of rivalry in the ranks. *I* have faith in you, but the other five—well. I'd like to put you in reserve for a bit."

Michelle was narked. Were the other Agents jealous? How was it *her* fault if she adjusted better to the time-jumps than they?

Her vexation must have shown on her face. Hera soothed, "Just have a break, recharge, and I'll see what I can do to have you back in the field sooner."

What could she say to that? "Thank you, Commissioner."

Michelle slept most of the space-flight back to Vivaldis, stumbled through Customs and caught a shuttle home.

"You're back!" her housemate Girion chirped, his fluoro pink dreadlocks bouncing as he bowed. "How was your study trip? Did you learn lots? What are Earth men like? Would I like them?"

Stifling a yawn, Michelle slung her bag onto the floor and flopped down on a chair. "Great. Yes. Just like Vivaldan men. Probably. Do you want to get

Rilaan for dinner? I have credit." She looked around the tiny apartment. Girion kept saying he'd redecorate, but when he wasn't out on dates he was studying hard for his astro-mechanics doctorate. She didn't care—she was hardly ever here. Telling him she went on study trips was the easiest explanation since her work was secret. She supposed she could afford her own apartment now that she worked for the Time-Space Agency, but frugality had been part of her nature for so long. Besides, it was nice to come home to a place that was friendly, if worn around the edges.

"Ohh! I'm meeting someone." Her friend was disappointed. Then his face lit. "Actually, you should come! His friend is into women but really shy, so we were going to help him pick up. But if you come, the two of you can chat." He winked. "Nice welcome home present for you."

"I'm pretty tired..." Michelle protested. "I was looking forward to a quiet night in."

"Don't be boring!" Girion bounded into his bedroom. "Have a quick nap, take a Pep-Up and put your dancing shoes on! It'll be grand!"

Michelle grumbled but went along with it. Her social life had been severely curtailed in the last year, once she'd started running missions for the Agency.

She was annoyed at how quickly Girion went off into the club with his new boyfriend and left her with Enargo. He was an amicable-looking fellow, with dark curly hair and bronze skin. Michelle envied him his colouring.

"So are you local?" she asked brightly, shrugging off her weariness.

"From Nuevos Aires," he smiled, naming a city on the other side of the planet. "And you?"

"Born right here in Vivaldis Prime."

"I'm studying at the University," he went on.

"Oh, I go there!" It was a lie—she'd graduated during her traineeship at the Time-Space Agency, but the cover for the secretive nature of her job was that she was doing post-graduate study in Earth history. "What do you study?"

"History," Enargo said. "And you?"

"History as well! What a coincidence." She leant forward and tapped the corner of her mouth. They would actually have something to talk about!

"Oh really?" He raised dark eyebrows. "What field? I haven't seen you in any of my classes."

Michelle caught the android barman's eye and signalled for service. An energising juice was in order—she didn't want to embarrass herself by yawning. "Earth History—everything from ancient right up to the intra-stellar age."

"Hmph." He didn't seem impressed. Not that she expected him to fall over with amazement but surely it was worth showing a little enthusiasm? How many people on a blind date got to meet someone who shared their field of interest? "That's really broad."

"I'm looking at long-term patterns in human society." The lie was polished, delivered smoothly.

"Oh. Well, I'm looking at specialising in twentieth-century Asian history. Asia is a geographical and cultural region of Earth that still supports the majority of the human population there. It was critical in pioneering colonist programs for our species to get off the planet."

"Yes, I know," Michelle grinned. "The twentieth century was a challenging time for many Asian countries. Lots of wars and new ideologies." She hoped he'd pick up that she'd said 'countries' not 'provinces' and twig that she well versed in the subject.

"Of course, Asia wasn't one homogenous province

like it is now." Enargo leant forward and Michelle shifted back. "It was divided into much smaller political divisions called 'countries'. The largest and most influential one was called China. We know Beijing to be the capital city of Earth, but back then it was only the capital city of China."

"I know," Michelle replied, a little confused. Even primary school kids knew that fact. Was he lecturing her? She'd hoped for an intellectual conversation. *It's not a competition on who knows the most.* Despite that thought, she couldn't help herself. "The rise of Japan as a military power and the subsequent clash with the rest of Asia and then the United States and allies is an interesting topic in that era."

She was being a smart-arse. One of her recent missions had involved the winding up of what was known as World War Two. She had failed to prevent the Nagasaki bombing, which had upset her badly, but one of her colleagues had managed to correct the timeline working through the Soviet side. The history that was now overwritten existed only in special computers in the Time-Space Agency on Vivaldis and Earth. Michelle had spent half her recovery time going over the new history of those weeks.

"Japan was a collection of densely populated islands to the east of China. During the twentieth century, they rose as a military power and invaded many other countries in Asia. They also declared war on the United States of America by bombing Pearl Harbour. Pearl Harbour was a naval base of the United States in a series of islands called Hawaii, in the Pacific Ocean..." He kept going.

Michelle was astounded. Had he swallowed an encyclopaedia program? He'd completely ignored what she'd said, instead seizing on the topic to prove his expertise. All keenness she'd felt for the evening evaporated. She stared across the dancefloor and sipped her juice as Enargo droned on.

Michelle was dying to tell him to shut up, he was boring the hell out of her, but her work training had rubbed off. She observed him and the people in the club. It was getting busy.

The music got louder. Enargo compensated by raising his voice.

*I know! I was there!* she screamed internally as he talked about how journalists and photographers changed history by bringing war into the living rooms of the Western World during the Vietnam conflict.

"Will you excuse me?" She stood abruptly. Enargo frowned, peering up at her. "I've just seen a friend of mine. I'll be right back." She wended her way through the crowd and skirted the dance floor, ducking between a laughing pair of blue-furred Mayash.

"Girion!" She yelled in her housemate's ear. "This date is a dud, I'm going home!"

"Bit of a stud? Don't stress, Shelly babe! I won't be home till tomorrow—apartment's all yours!" He winked and turned back to his boyfriend, who kissed him passionately.

Michelle growled then turned to spot Enargo honing in on her. *Crap, he's coming over.* She looked frantically for an escape. She launched herself over the bar and slid down past the juice dispensers. Several androids beeped warnings at her as she scooted past and burst out the door into the cool night air of the alley beyond.

The music from the club muffled now, she heaved a sigh of relief.

*First thing tomorrow I'm sending a com to Commissioner Hera requesting early termination of my leave.* She stepped out and headed towards the nearest monorail station. *I'd rather go back to work than go on another date!*

# SKULLS FOR WINGS
## Delia Strange

It was a new day and, for Reiko, a new life.

Beside her, a sleeping woman lay with her back turned. Her close-shaved head was unable to hide the small medi-plate affixed to her nape. Past the woman was a large, barred window revealing a strip of morning sky between tall, grey buildings. Faint blares of car horns filtered through the glass.

Reiko threw back the sheet and was surprised by a colourful tattoo that ran the length of her arm, featuring butterflies with skulls for wings. She stood up awkwardly from the mattress—it was set upon floorboards. There was no furniture in this room, but the walls were pasted with abstract posters of mournful people and clothes littered the floor. When the woman stirred, Reiko left the room by the closest door.

"Annie?" A sleep-drunk voice followed her into the bathroom. A pair of tights hung over the tub and a wad of blue hair choked the sink. Reiko thumbed the door latch and assessed herself in a bathroom mirror pitted with black spots.

Roughly cut blue hair framed a pale face with a pierced eyebrow and smudged makeup. The Company had chosen someone very different today.

The doorknob rattled as it was turned and then a fist pounded the door.

"Annie, what the fuck?"

The voice wasn't sleepy anymore.

A quick glance dismissed the window as too small to crawl out of. She didn't know what floor she was on and she was only wearing a singlet and underwear.

"I am making use of the toilet," Reiko explained when she spied the grimy lavatory.

"You're making use of the toilet?"

She had to match their speech patterns to avoid detection. Lovers often mimicked each other in such ways. She'd been greeted with profanity so took that cue.

"Fuck off."

The other woman grumbled but moved away. Reiko sat and emptied her bladder, knowing her options were limited. She had to bluff the woman long enough to get dressed and make her escape.

When Reiko exited the bathroom, the woman was pulling on a pair of tight red leather shorts. There was something similar on the floor nearby so she grabbed it and stepped into it. The shorts wouldn't move past her thighs. The expression on the other woman's face required more bluffing.

"Don't leave your shit on my side of the bed." Reiko punctuated her sentence by throwing the shorts at the woman's face, who swatted them aside.

"Annie, baby, are you still upset about last night?"

Reiko found some black jeans that looked wider at the hips and pulled them on. Success. There were boots nearby that she shoved her feet into. They fit also.

"We'll talk about it later."

"Stop putting me off," the woman complained. "I'm sorry I chickened out."

Reiko spared her a shrug before she left the room, this time using the door on the adjacent wall. It led her into a combined kitchen and living area. Moving quickly so she couldn't be challenged again, Reiko walked out the front door.

She stood in a beige hallway with peeling paint. There was a lingering smell of fish that grew stronger as she approached the stairwell. Behind her, a door opened.

"Annie? Where are you going?"

Reiko was annoyed by the pestering woman. What kind of controlling relationship was this Annie person in? She continued but was being followed. She had to stop this woman from interfering. The Company wouldn't like headlines about strange behaviour before a disappearance. It was no longer just conspiracy theorists who were noticing, but serious journalists.

She swung around before she could be grabbed.

"Leave me alone, I'm taking a walk."

Suspicion in the other woman's eyes alerted her to a wrong answer.

"You sound like you've been fucking Collected," the woman said uneasily. She seemed not to believe her own words but Reiko noticed her pupils had dilated. For this woman to accurately guess what was happening to her partner meant that this couple knew about the program.

"Because I'm not taking your shit anymore?" Reiko hazarded. It was also possible this woman was suspicious about her partner because she was always suspicious about her partner. Her words hit the mark, she could see hurt in the other woman's eyes... then, grim determination.

"What's my name, then?"

To use their word: Fuck.

Reiko bent her fingers, turning her hand into a stiff club rather than a fist, and jabbed it upward into the unknown woman's trachea. She felt soft flesh compress beneath her strike and a choked sound escaped the woman's lips before she fell backwards onto the dingy floor, clawing weakly at her throat. Reiko didn't look back.

The Company would see what had happened when they uploaded her data. Her options had been limited; they would commend her for preserving the discretion of the program.

Reiko scurried down eleven flights of stairs into a quiet foyer. She burst out through the front door and almost misstepped on the cement stairs leading to the pavement. Her flurry of activity was barely noticed by the crowd brushing past one another to get to their destinations.

Reiko had a destination of her own and a mission to complete before Annie's lover was found. The objectives had been programmed into her when she'd downloaded into Annie's brain through the medi-plate.

One day she would fail to upload herself back into the Company's servers. One day, she would find someone that she wanted to remain inside of. With a murdered woman outside Annie's apartment, her situation was too complicated.

But tomorrow would bring a new day and, for Reiko, a new life.

# OTHER BOOKS BY 1231 PUBLISHING

### WANDERER OF WORLDS
**Linda Conlon & Delia Strange**

A contemporary sci-fi fantasy series set in a multiverse where everybody is out for themselves. Wanderers shift between worlds using their powers while the Authorities hunt them down using giant mechanical portals.

### TURNING POINT SERIES
**Jodie Lane**

A time-travelling series about a young woman caught up in a plot to devastate future Earth. Starting with 'The Siege of Masada' and visiting other historical events and people, this series is packed with action and twists in history.

### FEMME: LIGHT
**Delia Strange**

The utopian world of Femme is a destination that empowers women, for all men are slaves. When Kaley from Earth arrives, she discovers that Femme's beauty is only skin deep.

### OBLIQUITY
**1231 Publishing**

The first of The Australian Pen short story collection explores the dark and twisting paths of corruption and deceit. None of these stories are what they first appear to be.

## www.1231publishing.com